HUNGRY

ALETHEA EASON

HUNGRY

An Imprint of HarperCollins*Publishers*

Eos is an imprint of HarperCollins Publishers.

Hungry
Copyright © 2007 by Alethea Eason
All rights reserved. Printed in the United States of America.
No part of this book may be used or reproduced in any manner whatsoever without
written permission except in the case of brief quotations embodied in critical articles and
reviews. For information address HarperCollins Children's Books, a division of
HarperCollins Publishers, 1350 Avenue of the Americas, New York, NY 10019.
www.harpercollinschildrens.com

Library of Congress Cataloging-in-Publication Data
Eason, Alethea.
Hungry / Alethea Eason. — 1st ed.
    p.   cm.
Summary: Deborah develops a crush on her best friend Willy, but she is not happy
when her alien parents tell her she must eat him for dinner.
ISBN 978-0-06-082554-6 (trade bdg.) — ISBN 978-0-06-082555-3 (lib. bdg.)
[1. Extraterrestrial beings—Fiction. 2. Best friends—Fiction. 3. Friendship—Fiction.
4. Science fiction.] I. Title.
PZ7.E126725Hu 2007   2007011594
[Fic]—dc22   CIP
                                                                                   AC

Typography by Al Cetta
1 2 3 4 5 6 7 8 9 10

First Edition

For Bill

Contents

One: Coffins in the Living Room 3

Two: The Bride Wore Black 10

Three: Hooked on Horror 23

Four: Eating the Logans 37

Five: Jackpot! 49

Six: Cruising the Casino 61

Seven: Mom Loses It 71

Eight: Alley-Oops 81

Nine: Forbidden Delights 89

Ten: Bathroom Issues 100

Eleven: Supper at Sho-Sho-Pah 111

Twelve: The Oasis 124

Thirteen: Don't Be Too Afraid 133

Fourteen: Purgation 140

Fifteen: Essence of Home 152

Sixteen: Math Champ 164

Seventeen: Dbkrrrsh 174

Eighteen: Tentacles 187

HUNGRY

Chapter One

Coffins in the Living Room

On the first day of school, Mr. Bartlett said algebra was good for us, the way protein was. I didn't know about that, but two months later, he was still droning on about the value of x, and my best friend Willy was slinking lower and lower in his seat. I'm good at math, and I knew I had to do something. That day at recess I offered to tutor him, but he just said, "Save yourself, Deborah, I'm a lost cause."

Nobody knows this, but Deborah's not even my name. It's just the closest in English to my real one, which is impossible for people to pronounce. Even I have trouble saying it. There were a lot of things Willy didn't know about me. He had no idea how weird my family was. So I just stuck to my plan: I told him to think of algebra as a language that used numbers instead of words. But my example was beyond him.

"Huh?" he said, and then ducked as a ball whizzed by his head.

"Freak," Alicia Henderson called out. She had deliberately kicked the ball at him.

It was October 1, the first day of Halloween, according to Willy. His family celebrated the holiday all month long, and he'd come to school in a vampire's cape to get into the spirit. I thought he was brave for wearing the cape thirty days before the main event. I also respected his conviction that he had the right to dress in a way that reflected his family's values, because Alicia wasn't the only one who gave him a hard time.

Alicia was skinny, all arms and legs, constantly spinning plots, thinking of ways to be the center of attention.

She and I had gone to school together since kindergarten, and she'd never been nice to me. Last year in fifth grade, Willy and his dad, Fred, moved to Prattville from Sacramento. When he started coming to school looking like the Wolf Man, Alicia was especially cruel. Sixth grade wasn't going to be any different.

Willy glared at her. If I didn't distract him, he'd be upset for the rest of the day, just what Alicia wanted.

"Never mind her," I said. "If you want help in math, I'll call my mom to see if it's okay for me to come to your house after school and help you with your homework."

I'm pretty stubborn, and I wasn't going to give up on my friend. Mr. Bartlett had told the class that on October fifteenth everyone was required to try out for the class team for the Math Champs contest that was to be held in January, whether they stank in math or not. (Okay, he didn't exactly use the word "stink.") One sixth grader every year was also awarded the Math Champ crown, and I just knew the award would belong to me.

Our class team would compete with teams from the other sixth grade classes. I wanted Willy to at least get through the first couple of rounds during the tryouts.

Willy still stared at Alicia.

"Hey, I asked you a question," I said, tapping him on his shoulder.

He looked back at me, the scowl fading from his face. "Oh, sure, Deborah, you could finally meet Margie."

Margie was Willy's dad's girlfriend. She'd just quit her job in Sacramento and moved in with them.

Mom said that going to Willy's was fine. She was putting together a huge Avon order and this would give her time to deliver it. I just had to be home by four-thirty.

That afternoon on the way to his house, Willy said, "No one else knows this yet, but Dad and Margie are getting married. Guess where?"

"Where?"

"In the cemetery at ten minutes before midnight on Halloween. Isn't that cool?"

"I guess?" I said, trying to be polite.

Fred's video store had the biggest horror-movie collection in Northern California, including some really rare old ones. Still, the wedding sounded bizarre. Wasn't Fred taking this interest a little too far?

Even stranger was what I saw as I walked into his living room. The couch was gone. Instead, three coffins were lined up in front of the television set. Each had a big pillow for a backrest.

I could tell which coffin was Willy's right away; it was the shortest.

"What are these?" I asked.

"They're for Halloween." Willy grinned. "Margie thought of it when she found out we have cousins who are undertakers. We're using them to watch TV." Then he saw the look on my face and got defensive. "They're comfortable, Deborah. It's a shame to waste them on the dead."

Since it was a nice day, we went out to the patio. Margie brought us a plate of chocolate-chip cookies. I didn't take one, hoping I didn't appear rude. Unfortunately a loud growl came from my midsection.

"Have some cookies, Deborah," Margie told me, offering me the plate.

"She can't," Willy said. "She has a lot of allergies and can only eat these weird green wafers."

I nodded and pulled one out of my pocket to show to her. I bit into it and felt it fizz in my mouth, which did nothing to curb my appetite.

"Oh, that is a shame," Margie said. "You must have a very delicate system."

If she only knew how wrong she was.

I had expected Margie to be dark and mysterious, so I was disappointed that she seemed to be the standard mom type, a little chubby, with a bright, cheerful smile. The only thing that gave away her fondness for the season was a pair of skeleton earrings that hung down to her shoulders. But, heck, our school secretary had some just like them.

"Willy's mentioned you're a whiz in math, Deborah," Margie said. "Thanks for the homework help."

"Not a problem," I said, as she pulled a chair onto the lawn and opened a magazine.

After ten minutes, I started thinking Willy might be a lost cause. He only knew his times table to the sixes, and he wasn't that certain about six times eight.

After the last problem, Willy grabbed another cookie

off the plate and asked, "So, what are you writing your book report on? Mine's about dirt bikes."

"You always write about dirt bikes when we have to read nonfiction," I told him. "I'm reading a book about immigration."

"Why?" Willy asked.

He leaned on his elbows expectantly. His eyes were pale blue and his red hair curled above the collar of his cape. I'd never noticed this before, but Willy Logan was actually cute.

"Immigration is an important topic." Margie's voice brought me back to reality. "Except for Native Americans, we're all immigrants in this country."

I felt myself grow red. I guess you could say my family were illegal immigrants. After coming to Prattville, my family had "assimilated" (a word on next Friday's spelling test), and the government didn't know we were here.

I looked like an ordinary preteen: short blond hair with bangs, average height. No one in my family would stand out in a crowd. We never had people over, in case they decided to get nosy. I never had a slumber party. My mom sold Avon door-to-door or on the telephone but didn't have clients come to our house. The people who work in Dad's office never stopped by, and he never took them up on their invitations to have a beer after work.

We couldn't just hide away completely, though, so we had ways of coping. For one thing, when we came to America, the last name we chose was Jones. How much more white-bread could we get than that?

Also, though my parents and I spoke English flawlessly,

we made sure we didn't go around saying things like "It is I," or "To whom do you wish to speak?" We stuck to your everyday West Coast American way of talking.

Actually, we spoke several other languages, including Chinese, and that's one thing we did keep secret. Mom said the languages would come in handy when the others arrived.

When I got home, my parents were shut up in the den. Their voices were muffled, but my dad sounded angry.

"It's time!" I heard him shout.

Mom was arguing with him, but I couldn't make out what she was saying. I sat at the breakfast bar and pretended I was reading my social studies book. What was so great about Egyptian dynasties that lasted only a few hundred years? Back home, we had ten-thousand-year dynasties, and we were still going strong.

When my parents came into the kitchen, Dad's face was red, the way it gets when he's upset.

"Anything wrong?" I asked.

"Yes," said Dad.

"No," said Mom at the same time.

"We'll explain later," Dad said. "I'm glad to see you've finally discovered the importance of homework."

That wasn't fair because I *always* did my homework. He began lecturing for the 127th time about how I would use what I learned in school to become a leader among our kind.

I needed to get his attention.

"Uh, Dad . . ."

I pointed to his head.

One of his tentacles had popped out. They do that sometimes when he gets agitated. He reached up and shoved it back in. Mom doesn't let him out of the house without a hat.

Chapter Two

The Bride Wore Black

The fifteenth of Halloween came. Willy had begun to date his papers this way, and I was growing hungrier.

Mr. Bartlett had grown more and more irritated at Willy, who was adding something ghoulish to his wardrobe every few days. Willy now wore the Dracula cape with one of Margie's skeletons dangling from an earlobe. His hair was frizzed as though he'd stuck a finger in a light socket, and he'd painted his fingernails black. They were especially long because he hadn't cut them since July.

Right after the pledge, Mr. Bartlett noticed how Willy had written the date on top of his practice spelling test. "I've told you to stop doing that," he said.

He should have made his living selling shoes instead of working with children. At least pairs of sneakers don't have feelings.

A silly grin crossed Willy's face. I knew that look: he was nervous. My first thought was *Uh-oh, Willy's going to get in trouble,* followed quickly by *Why haven't I noticed how long his eyelashes are before?*

"My dad says it's my constitutional right to celebrate Halloween in any way I believe."

With Willy's words, a hush fell over the class. All morning Alicia had been acting as though her new braces were the start of a fashion trend. She flashed a mean silver smile and then leaned over her desk and whispered to her friend Amanda, "Freak."

Mr. Bartlett ignored Alicia. Her father was on the school board, and she could get away with anything in his class. He walked over to Willy's desk, tore up his paper. "Tell your father that excuse doesn't work in my classroom. Remove those items now," Mr. Bartlett ordered, "and comb your hair."

Willy crossed his arms like a true rebel. "I have the right to wear what I want. It's guaranteed in the Bill of Rights."

"My classroom is not a democracy. Take those things off, or you'll go to the principal's office."

Willy stood up with more dignity than I thought possible, considering how he was dressed, flung his backpack over his shoulder, and walked out of the room.

A huge growl echoed out of my stomachs and spread through the room. Alicia snickered again. I wanted to be anywhere in the universe other than Room 36 of Prattville Elementary School.

Willy was suspended for the rest of the day. The Math Champs tryouts were held in the afternoon. I answered every question correctly and got on the math team, like I knew I would. Unfortunately so did Alicia.

After school I went to Willy's house to see how he was doing.

"The school won't let Willy come back if he wears his costume," Margie said as she opened the door.

"They didn't care last year," I told her.

"The principal says there's a new policy to strictly enforce the dress code," Margie said. "Willy's going back to school tomorrow in his regular clothes, but we've decided to start fighting for next year."

Willy's dad was sitting in one of the coffins, talking on the telephone. He waved when he saw me. The living room was now draped with spiderwebs, and plastic bats hung from the ceiling.

"Fred's phoning the American Civil Liberties Union to see if we can get a lawyer to argue our case," Margie said. She was beginning to look more like how I'd imagined her before we'd met. Her long black dress rustled as she led me to the kitchen.

"What does that mean?" I asked.

"The ACLU is a group that helps to defend people who feel their rights have been taken away. We're protesting Willy not being allowed to celebrate Halloween in the way we feel is meaningful."

Willy was at the counter, working on his nonfiction book report. A book about the *Titanic* was splayed open in front of him.

"No dirt bikes?" I asked.

Willy shrugged. "Margie says I have to get out of my comfort zone."

I smiled, but then I said seriously, "Sorry about what happened."

He shrugged again. "Are you on the team?"

I nodded. "With Chen and Alicia."

Willy wrinkled his nose. "At least Chen's okay." Then

he surprised me. "Do you think your parents would let you come to the wedding?"

"I'm invited?"

"Your whole family can come if they want," Margie called from her coffin.

Walking home, I wondered how I could talk my parents into going to the wedding. The night in question was a little dicey, but I figured they might be able to fit it into their plans.

To my surprise, Dad said he'd be delighted to go, but he was so hungry a tentacle popped out. I should have figured out he had big plans for Halloween.

The big day was on a Saturday. Willy called me early in the morning to say the cake had just arrived. The frosting was black and there was a vampire bride and groom on top.

"I'm going trick-or-treating before we leave for the cemetery. Want to come along?"

"I'm sorry. I can't make it." I said.

Before we left for the wedding, Mom called me into her bedroom. Since it was Halloween, I wasn't surprised she let her tentacles protrude. My family doesn't have a thing for the holiday, but it's convenient for us. Our metabolism is slow, so we need to feed only once a year. Since people think we're in costume, we use the night to our advantage.

I've never liked the idea of eating people, but it's what we had to do to survive. Once I got started and felt their essences in my bloodstream, I couldn't stop until I gorged myself. (Essence is the fear people experience right before we eat them.)

Our species has six tentacles, so we can devour our prey while defending ourselves against others. It's one of the evolutionary adaptations that helped us conquer vast regions of space.

We have slits on top of our heads that are so thin they're microscopic, but at feeding time they open so our tentacles can push out. Sometimes our tentacles pop out all by themselves when we get emotional. Mom taught me how to control this when I was little, but Dad has a harder time. Mom says males, in general, have more difficulty with this.

All six tentacles connect with one esophagus. We use what humans would call our "normal" mouths to feed as well. There's an old saying on the Home World: *Seven mouths are better than six.*

Mom and Dad had always gone out and brought food back for me, but now Mom told me that Dad had decided that I was old enough to hunt for myself. She said she wanted to protect me a little longer, but she had to accept that I was growing up.

As far as I was concerned, the idea stunk.

"But, Mom, I don't want to hunt people. It's bad enough I have to eat them. I just want to eat chicken or nachos like everybody else."

"You know eating those things would kill you." Mom sounded alarmed, like I'd told her I was planning to take drugs. I kept pouting, so she kept talking. "I know how fond you are of the humans. To tell the truth, hunting gets harder for me each year. Earthlings can be so endearing. But your dad reminded me that the rest of us will be here soon."

"He says that every year."

"I know, Dbkrrrsh." A tentacle reached out and stroked my hair.

She'd used my real name, something my parents rarely did because they wanted to be sure they didn't slip up in public. I thought of them more as George and Virginia than Grrgg and Vgnrlk. Our language doesn't have vowels, and though I understand it perfectly, I have a heck of a time with pronunciation.

Mom continued. "You know your father is right. When the rest do get here and we've conquered the planet, there won't be any room to be sentimental."

"But, Mom, that's no way for a democracy to work."

"For goodness' sakes, Deborah, you ought to know by now that the Home World is not a democracy."

Her words brought Mr. Bartlett to mind. I was going to suggest we eat him, but then it dawned on me what Dad was planning, why he was so thrilled about going to the wedding.

"Mom, I don't want to eat Willy's family."

Mom crossed two of her tentacles. "Sweetie, before long you're going to have to do a lot of things you don't like."

For most of the year, I tried not to think of our feeding frenzy, about what I had to do to survive. But when Mom and Dad brought dinner home each Halloween, my DNA took over and I ate until the sun came up. You'd be surprised by how much meat an eleven-year-old girl has to consume to be sustained for a year. I needed at least one full-grown adult all to myself. If there were leftovers from my parents, I never refused second helpings.

What our bodies needed, what we really thrived on, was the essence of a person. To be truly nourished, we needed to feed on creatures fully aware of what was happening. Their fear and their sense of betrayal gave us chemical reactions that not only felt great but also were like vitamins. Or so I'd been told.

After a few days, feedings always seemed like they never happened, at least until I got hungry the following October. Up until now, it wasn't personal. I never ate anyone I knew.

"We've always eaten the homeless so there's less of a chance of getting caught," I said. "So why are we going to devour a whole wedding party?"

Mom was silent for a moment and studied her hands. "Your father thinks it's a risk we must take." She raised her head and looked at me sternly. "Deborah, we want you to eat Willy."

"But, Mom . . ."

"If you can eat him, you can eat anybody, which is exactly what will be expected now that you're almost a young lady."

"No way!" I screamed. "You can't make me eat my best friend."

I ran to my room and slammed my door. Then I turned over the picture on my dresser, taken just before we left the Home World, of my parents holding me as a newborn, before our bodies were modified to fit in on Earth. My Earth-skin, what we called our overskin, grew with me, and my parents aged appropriately. Dad was getting white temples, and Mom had started using Avon's antiaging products. Underneath, though, we were all gloppy and green. I hated how we really looked, and I hated what we were.

I sulked all evening, but my hunger pangs were so

intense my belly had started to control my brain. I needed food, and soon. My resolve was breaking down, but I wasn't going to admit that to my parents.

At 11:20, Dad banged on my door.

"It's time to go, and if you don't leave your room this minute, young lady, you're grounded."

"Okay, I'm coming already," I shouted, running a brush through my hair. "But if Willy is going to be some-one's dinner, he's not going to be mine."

When we got to the cemetery, my parents took both of my elbows and marched me to where a small crowd was gathering. The theme of the wedding seemed to be vampires.

I felt out of place with my tentacles sticking up through my head, dressed like a geek in one of my mom's old silver jumpsuits that she used to wear back home. I had to roll up the pant legs because they were too long. Worse yet, both Mom and Dad wore suits that matched mine.

There were about ten guests besides us, more people than we actually needed to satisfy our hunger. We'd be breaking out the Rolaids (the one thing on Earth that our systems didn't reject) before sunrise.

Willy's job was to welcome the guests. He was also going to be his dad's best man. He looked nice in his tuxedo with his hair slicked back. The white makeup and fangs became him.

My stomachs started to rumble. I closed my eyes for a second, to steady myself. I knew once I got a whiff of essence, there would be no way I'd be able to control myself. *Don't eat Willy, don't eat Willy,* I told myself.

Just then, he walked up to us. "Great costumes. Look,

we're about to start. Catch me after the wedding."

"Sure thing," I said. "We're planning on it."

A funeral march drifted eerily over the gravestones. My parents and I stood off to the side of the other guests, waiting until it was time to make our move. Willy and his dad stood with a minister, the only person not in costume, underneath a black awning that had MARGIE AND FRED, FOREVER written on it in bloodred fluorescent paint that sparkled in the moonlight.

Margie glided out of a crypt wearing a black lace wedding gown and a veil made out of diaphanous webbing. She carried a bouquet of black lilies. Everyone let out a sigh.

The ceremony began. Fred and Margie had written their own vows, all about loving and cherishing and promising to haunt the other when death did them part. All the guests closed in, and I knew that as soon as they kissed my parents were going to pounce.

Out of the corner of my eye I saw one of Dad's tentacles hover over the old guy next to me. I could see the three rows of Dad's serrated teeth. My tentacles rose with my mother's as I felt the memories of my ancestors feeding deep within my body.

Just then a floodlight hit us, and our tentacles withdrew like lightning. A voice boomed from a bullhorn.

"Just what do you think you're doing there?"

For a moment I thought we'd been caught, but Willy's family had just forgotten to get a permit for the use of the cemetery. Police were everywhere. I could see Fred and Margie talking to an officer, pointing at the cake. It took several minutes, but the police finally let them finish the ceremony.

A little while later, everyone, including the police, was eating wedding cake. Everyone but us, that is. My parents and I hadn't fed, and I was literally shaking from hunger.

I couldn't help what happened next. Mom said it's because I'm growing, and when I have to eat, I have to eat. The night was dark, and one of the policemen walked back to his car alone. The parking lot was over a knoll, and I was pretty sure no one could see.

I followed. My tentacles encircled him, and I began to feed. Down the hatch went bones, clothes, shoelaces. Some thread from his uniform got stuck in my teeth. I was going to have to floss seven sets of teeth—one set per tentacle and what you'd call my regular ones—but I didn't care. His essence, the wonderful taste of fear, flowed through my veins.

But before I consumed even half of him, my parents found me. As they finished him off, I felt like saying, "Hey, get your own meal," but I knew they wanted to get out of the parking lot pronto.

Driving home, Dad burped and said, "That's my girl."

Mom, though, scolded me. "You could have put our whole mission at risk."

Dad patted her hand. "No harm done. No one saw anything."

"I wish I could be as confident as you," Mom said, but she dropped the subject.

We hadn't been home for more than ten minutes when a policeman knocked on our door. Mom had just enough time to throw a hat on Dad's head. It bobbled a bit, but the policeman didn't notice.

"Excuse me," he said, "but one of our officers is missing. I'm just checking to see if all the guests have gotten home safely."

"Ah, yes, we did," Dad told him.

"Did you see anything out of the ordinary?" The policeman chuckled. "Other than the wedding, that is."

"We actually left early and didn't stay for the reception. It was way past our daughter's bedtime."

The policeman asked a couple more questions and then seemed satisfied.

By the time he left, I was ready for bed. There was just one problem. "I'm still hungry," I said.

Dad kissed me good night. "Sweetie," he said, "something will work out."

Sunday morning we had a family talk. Mom repeated what she had said the afternoon before: Eating my human friends was going to be expected of me. I couldn't show any favoritism.

"You've tasted fear," Mom said. "But you've never tasted fear and betrayal together."

Dad closed his eyes and smacked his lips. "Absolutely delicious."

"What we're trying to say is that we think once you've taken a few bites, you'll enjoy the experience."

I looked out the kitchen window. One policeman, even a chubby one, among the three of us just hadn't been enough. My stomachs still hurt.

"Dbkrrrsh," Dad said, using his slightly stern voice. I looked at him reluctantly. "If the opportunity presents itself again, it's your duty to your species not to be sentimental. Do you understand?"

"Besides," Mom said, "I can't tell you how much it would advance our careers if the Supreme High Council found out we had raised a daughter willing to eat a school chum. I'm talking about your future as well. Who knows how high you could rise someday if you prove that you're merciless to the Earthlings?"

I guess it may be hard to imagine an eleven-year-old needing to think so seriously about a career, but my parents taught me from the time I was born what happened to families who weren't on the Home Planet fast track. Your status determined your feeding order, and even "old" families like ours could fall from favor and starve to death.

Duty. Career. Two words for my species that had almost as strong a pull as feeding. They had me. I reluctantly nodded in agreement.

Before school started on Monday, Willy ran up to me on the playground. "Thanks for coming to the wedding," he said. "I looked for you after the ceremony."

"My parents wanted to get me home."

"Weird about that policeman, huh? They still haven't found him."

My stomachs growled at the thought. "Yeah, weird."

The bell rang, and we walked to class together.

"Hey, Margie wants to know if you and your folks would like to come over for Thanksgiving dinner," Willy said as we lined up.

At that moment I made a decision that I hated. Duty and career. How many worlds had my species conquered marching to those words? I had all of our history screaming at me about what was the right thing to do.

I forced my heart to harden as my stomachs rumbled once more. The invasion was a certainty. If Willy was going to be eaten anyway, I could try to make it as easy as possible for him, take him by surprise before he knew anything was going to happen. What I'd lose in essence, I'd make up for with not hating myself quite as much.

"We'd be glad to come," I said, quickly wiping away a tear. We cry red tears, so crying was another challenge, another thing we tried not to do in front of humans. "Tell her we'll bring dessert."

Chapter Three

Hooked on Horror

The memory of how the policeman tasted, how extra chewy he was, wouldn't let go of me. "Probably the doughnuts," my dad said. My cravings drove me crazy, but my stomachs were in knots over the Thanksgiving meal at the Logans'.

So, would my parents pounce on Willy's parents first? And then would they insist I do the same thing with Willy? Who would be the second course? Margie's dad?

I asked Mom about this, and she said, "We'll improvise like we always do. Mother always said feeding is an art form."

I knew my grandmother was bloodthirsty, but this was the first time I heard she had a creative side as well. My grandmother was supposedly famous for being especially pitiless. She'd been held up as a role model for as long as I could remember, and when she came to Earth she'd expect the same ruthlessness from me.

Mom insisted that I practice saying Grandmother's name. As I've mentioned, languages come easy to me. *Je parle français très bein. Hablo español como una nativa.*

Nihongo o hanashimasu? Why, yes, as a matter of fact, I do speak Japanese.

My only problem is that the Home World language is hard for me to get my tongue around. I understand it when I hear it, but have you ever talked without using vowels? My parents were more than a little worried that I might not make a good first impression, another reason for me to make points with Grandmother over Willy.

"Say your grandmother's name again," Mom coached me once on our way back from Home Depot.

"Pags bat, Pugs bet, Pigs bait," I tried.

"Slowly. No vowels. P . . . g . . . s . . . b . . . t . . . t . . . k."

I tried again. This time "Pig's Butt" shot out of my mouth.

Mom pulled the car over and turned off the ignition.

"Dear, I'm sure your grandmother is well aware of all the domesticated farm animals of Earth. If you call her a Pig's Butt, and she decides to have you executed, I won't be able to do anything about it."

At school, Mr. Bartlett droned on day after day about algebraic equations. Willy wasn't the only kid who was lost. A lot of the kids *still* hadn't gotten the concept. I imagined eating them in order of their lack of aptitude in math: Amanda was the worst and then Thomas. Put together, they'd be hardly a snack back home, but I knew that with the first little nibble, the crunch of a pinkie or a toe in my mouth, I'd be out of control.

Chen, Alicia, and I were working on harder equations at the back table. All our lessons were now different from the rest of the class's in preparation for Math

Champs. If x = 12 and y = .5, what is the product of 4 (x + y)?

I watched Chen write down 48 + 2, and a bit of saliva dripped down my chin. As I wiped it off, I realized that Willy was the third worst student in math. I resolved once again to eat him for my parents' careers, as well as my own.

I had slowly accepted that Willy would be history, or at least social studies, after the twenty-third. Willy, Margie, and Fred were going to be turkey, potatoes, and pumpkin pie all wrapped up together. His grandparents and a couple of older cousins were visiting from out of town. By the time my parents and I were done eating, our bellies would bulge, and we'd have to waddle home. We'd be in a stupor, and my dad might even miss the ball games.

We'd be sated for another year, and we'd all be sane again.

Willy mouthed "Boring" from across the room and brought me back to the lesson. His smile seemed to flutter straight into my heart.

I let out a big groan.

"Is something bothering you, Deborah?" Mr. Bartlett asked, tapping his dry erase marker on the board. He was extra testy today, but maybe he was as frustrated with the class's lack of aptitude as I was about my feelings for Willy.

I shook my head and slumped down in my seat. I was the only alien in sixth grade. The only eleven-year-old alien girl alive on the planet. The only kid on Earth who was going to be forced to gorge on her best friend in just twelve days, and for the first time in her life she had a crush.

Not on any boy. Not Chen. Not Thomas. But on weird Willy Logan, her pal, the one she was going to make into chop suey.

Funny what a crush will do to a girl.

I decided that I might as well help Willy out in the meantime. Maybe he'd even get a C on the next test if I continued tutoring him. It was the least I could do.

During P.E., I asked him, "Do you want any more help in math?"

He didn't have to think twice. "Sure," and then his voice got a little edgy. "How did you get so smart, anyway?"

"Genetics."

"Yeah, right," Willy said.

The next morning Mr. Bartlett announced to the class that a miracle had occurred. Willy Logan had not only turned in his book report the day it was due, but had also gotten a B- on it. But then he added, "I doubt Willy will pull something like this off a second time." It took all my concentration not to let one of my tentacles shoot out and snap off his head.

It was Tuesday, and we had band practice that afternoon. On the way to the band room, Willy said, "Mr. Bartlett thinks I can't do it again? I'll show him."

"You know, Willy, you shouldn't let him bug you so much. Sixth grade won't last forever." The last words were out of my mouth before I knew what I was saying.

Band practice wasn't any easier for him. Willy loved to jam with his saxophone, playing riffs and improvising, but reading music and following along with the rest of the band weren't his strengths. Mr. Spencer, our band teacher, stopped us three times because Willy was either ahead or behind.

After he'd dragged his hands through his hair in frustration several times, Mr. Spencer was starting to look like Beethoven. None of us was playing well that day, including me.

I play the clarinet, and I like it a lot. The only problem was that in band I was first chair and Alicia was first second and had to sit next to me. We even had to share music. She'd challenged me three times in fifth grade, but each time when she got to the sixteenth notes she froze up and squeaked.

Today I was so busy thinking about how unfairly Mr. Bartlett had treated Willy that *I* squeaked on the high notes.

Mr. Spencer held up his hands as though he were beseeching the sky. "Hormones . . . Every year, it's the same thing with this grade, hormones."

Boy, was he burning out! But was there more going on between my classmates than I knew?

We muddled through "My Favorite Things" until it was time to put away our instruments. As Alicia broke down her clarinet, she turned toward the sax section and I swear she winked at Willy.

Why would she do that? Was she setting him up to tease him later? Then I looked down at her feet where she'd put her binder. On the cover she'd drawn a big heart with a pink pen and right in the middle was Willy's name, the "i" dotted with a smaller heart.

"I thought you hated Willy," I said, pointing to the notebook.

"Haven't you been paying attention?" she asked in a

stage whisper. "The rest of the girls have decided he's the cutest boy in sixth grade."

I wasn't alone in my feelings for Willy?

"No one asked my opinion," I said.

"Oh, Deborah, really. Everyone knows you're Willy's *friend*," Alicia dragged out the word "friend" a ridiculously long time, "not his girlfriend. Let's just say that I've changed my mind about him."

Was Alicia so shallow that she sold out her own conviction that Willy was a freak? Did human hormones do this to a person? Did she actually want to be his girlfriend?

By the time Willy and I walked to his house after school, I was almost frothing at the mouth thinking about what she'd said. As we turned onto his street, I finally got the courage to ask, "What do you think about Alicia?"

"Tin teeth?"

"I mean, do you think she could be somebody's girlfriend?"

"Huh?"

Willy had the same expression on his face as he did when I talked about algebra being a language.

"You didn't hear what she said after practice today about the cutest boy in sixth grade?" I asked.

Both of us stopped walking.

He shook his head, and then asked stupidly, "So, who is it?"

"You," I said, stomping my foot.

Willy shuddered. "Me? You've got to be joking, Deborah."

"You didn't see her wink at you?"

"I thought she had something in her eye."

We were both at a loss for words and didn't say anything to each other the rest of the way to his house.

Inside, the Halloween decorations had been taken down, but the coffins were permanent fixtures in the living room. I was used to them by now. The last time I was over I'd even sat in Willy's. He was right. The coffin was comfy, especially with a pillow propped up in back.

We put our books on the coffee table. "Good news," Margie called. We followed her voice into the kitchen. A flyer for a horror movie festival with a picture of Lon Chaney as Frankenstein's monster hung on the refrigerator.

"Wow," I said, reading the small print next to the picture. "This movie was made in 1933. That was a long time ago."

Margie leaned against the sink, writing a grocery list. "We especially like the old ones. When I saw *Frankenstein* on TV as a kid, I got hooked on horror."

She added something to the list and sighed happily. "Willy's dad and I met at a horror festival in Sacramento last summer. On our first date we found out how much we had in common. When we decided to get married, we both knew what we wanted, a wedding in a cemetery on Halloween."

Margie smiled dreamily, and I thought about how the elm trees that night had looked all lacy in the moonlight.

"Your wedding was beautiful," I told her.

She smiled. "I just had to wait until I found the right man."

Mom talked about Dad like that. She said she wanted to marry a man who liked to travel. And so here we were two hundred thousand light-years from home. Earth was considered a hardship post, but my parents had adjusted. She and Dad had even taken up golf.

"I'm starving," Willy said. "I think I'll make a sandwich."

"Would you like one, too?" Margie asked me.

"No, thanks," I said.

She tore off the paper she was writing on from the pad and looked at me strangely. "You never eat anything but those wafers?"

My stomachs gurgled as soon as she asked. She and Willy must have heard them.

"No," I said, crossing my arms over my belly defensively. "But they're really nutritious. My mom makes them herself. Did you know that she's an Avon Lady?"

Willy put peanut butter on a piece of bread and squished it into sandwich form.

"You want to get started?" he asked.

I could feel a tentacle start to rise out of my head. I pulled it in quickly. What was happening to me? I always had great tentacle control.

I nodded. It appeared he'd forgotten our entire conversation about Alicia. We sat at the breakfast bar and opened our math books. I talked him through the equations until we just had the extra credit problem at the end.

"Oh, good," I said. "I love word problems."

"You are so weird," Willy said. "So, what's the first step?"

For the first time that day, I was having fun, not like when I got home and had to answer stupid social studies questions.

Fred came home from work to grab a bite to eat

before the evening rush of customers. I hadn't realized it had gotten so late. Willy showed Fred his math paper while I gathered my things.

"Great job, son." His dad tousled his hair.

"Thanks, Dad," Willy said, and smiled at me the same way he did in class. The five chambers of my heart did little somersaults.

"It's so good to know Willy has a friend like you," Fred said sincerely. "Our family is a little different from most in this town and his other friends don't come around."

Willy looked peeved. "They're not allowed to visit us."

"Well, it's not always easy to be different," Margie said. "But in the long run you'll be glad you were brought up to be an individual."

She sounded just like my mom.

"The ACLU called about Willy's school, Fred," Margie continued, pouring glasses of iced tea for the three of them. "The lawyer said they'll represent us and that he thought the trial might happen sooner rather than later."

"Fantastic," I said. "This is good news, right?"

Mr. Logan drank a sip of tea, wiped his mouth, and said, "You bet. Serves them right."

My stomachs gurgled loudly again, and I said, "Got to run. I'll see you tomorrow, Willy."

I saw the little lines around Margie's eyes crinkle into worry marks. "See you soon, Deborah."

As it turned out, my parents hadn't noticed the time. Mom and Dad were in the garage fiddling with the communication controls. Dad had bought a 1966

Chevy Impala Super Sport convertible on eBay when I was in third grade. He said it was a classic, real vinyl interior, burgundy red paint job. Not only was it a cool car, but my parents had also turned it into an interstellar radio.

In August we'd received yet another report about an insurgent group that rumors said had followed us to Earth from the Home World. We'd gotten these messages on and off for as long as I could remember. My parents said it was a conspiracy theory and that there was no evidence there were rebels either back there or here, but they dutifully reported that they were on alert for signs of suspicious activity.

Lately my parents had been hush-hush about some of the messages we'd been receiving. That afternoon there must have been sunspots or something because when I came in Mom was standing on the hood of the car in her stockings. Dad was particular about not getting any scratches on the paint, but when reception was bad it was the only way they could transmit.

"Oh, hello, dear," Mom said between the antenna wire she held in her teeth. Her tentacles stood straight up for better reception.

"Hi. I did my math at Willy's," I said. "I just have social studies left."

"That's nice," Mom said.

"Have they fattened up with all that candy and wedding cake?" Dad joked.

"Not funny, Dad."

He chuckled. "Well, I think that's about it."

I leaned over and looked at the lights blinking across the dashboard.

"What do the lights mean?" I asked.

Dad stood up and stretched. "Sweetheart, I guess it's time to tell you. It looks like the rest are finally on their way."

"You're kidding? They're really coming?" I asked.

"My biggest worry is being put to rest as we speak," Dad said.

Mom jumped down to the garage floor. "You'll be able to mate with a nice boy from home," she said.

So far, holding hands with Willy was as much as I'd thought about. I hadn't even considered kissing. And now I was supposed to mate with a total stranger?

"Yuck," I said. "Someone I've never met?"

"He comes from a very good family," Mom said, taking me by the arm and escorting me into the house.

"I'm only eleven, Mom."

"And when are girls and boys considered adults, and when are they usually betrothed?" Mom asked like I was a first grader.

"Twelve," I said grudgingly.

"The actual mating doesn't happen until you're at least eighteen, so you can take that sour look off your face," Mom said. She turned to Dad and asked, "If we're going to have houseguests, have you thought where they're going to sleep?"

"What houseguests?" I asked.

"The first team will be staying with us, at least until they get their bearings," Dad said. "We could get a hide-a-bed for the den. Deborah could sleep on the couch in the living room if we needed her room."

"No way," I protested. "I'm not giving up my room."

"Deborah, we have to be hospitable," Mom said. "We

couldn't ask them to stay at the Holiday Inn, for goodness' sakes."

"Give up your own room," I muttered. "And I'll choose the person I want to marry, thank you very much."

My parents ignored me. Mom hugged my dad. "This is so exciting, George. Do you think we can get the new carpet laid before they arrive?"

I absolutely hated the fact that I might be engaged. My parents had ruined my entire life. I pouted until I got to school the next day and heard that Willy got an A- on his math test, a much more pleasant shock.

Mr. Bartlett was convinced Willy had cheated. His face grew red. "There's no way you could have gotten this grade. How did you do it?"

"I studied," Willy said, but unfortunately the way he said the words sounded like he was offering an excuse.

A spattering of giggles ran through the class, and Willy looked so mad that he could have been a member of my species just then.

"You're not being fair," I said in Willy's defense.

"Pardon me?" Mr. Bartlett's eyes narrowed.

"Willy didn't cheat. He didn't have to."

"And why is that?" he asked. He started to head in my direction.

"Because I tutored Willy, and I know how hard he's worked to bring up his grade."

The whole class giggled now. I wanted to devour all of them right then and there.

Mr. Bartlett was so close, I could smell his breath. Did he ever brush? "Are you saying I made a mistake?"

I wasn't going to let him bully me.

"You're always picking on Willy, and it's not fair."

My teacher's face was even redder than before, and he seemed to have forgotten all about Willy. "I will see you after school."

I wasn't going to back down. "You should give him the grade he deserves."

"Now you're telling me how to run my class? Detention until Thanksgiving."

I didn't care if I had detention for the next millennium.

I turned my head away from him and stared out of the window. The ships couldn't land soon enough. I wanted out of this place.

"Now get out your social studies books," Mr. Bartlett barked.

Willy had calmed down. As Mr. Bartlett turned to write on the board, he passed me a note.

Deborah,
Thanks. You're the best friend I ever had.
Willy

When the bell rang, everyone grabbed their backpacks and headed out the door. Alicia bumped me on purpose, but Willy gave me a thumbs-up as he left the room. I leaned back in my chair and stared at the little holes pressed into the ceiling tiles.

Mr. Bartlett placed a pile of his famous detention worksheets he always kept on hand in front of me and then sat down at his desk to grade papers. I reached into my desk and took out my silent reading book.

He didn't even look up.

"You're not here to enjoy yourself. Put that book down and start working on those vocabulary pages."

I slammed the book closed. I picked up a pencil and gnawed on the eraser. Thanksgiving was six whole days away. I didn't know how I was going to last.

Mr. Bartlett was bent over his papers so that his bald spot was like a beckoning target. It would be so easy. The custodians wouldn't be around for at least another hour, and by that time I could clean up whatever mess I might make.

Mr. Bartlett looked like he'd be kind of stringy, not as tasty as the policeman. He was constantly telling us the virtues of raw food. Still, it sure would be good to have full stomachs again.

My tentacles began to extend until all six were a foot out of my head. Drops of drool fell on my desk, smearing the three synonyms I'd just written for the word *happy*—joyful, cheerful, ecstatic—describing exactly how I'd feel once Mr. Bartlett was in my stomachs.

But then Mr. Bartlett cleared his throat, and I lost my nerve. My parents would probably smell his essence on my breath when I got home. I was going to have to wait until my species arrived.

Chapter Four

Eating the Logans

When I walked into the house, Mom was on the phone.

"I appreciate your concern, Mrs. Logan," she was saying. "But we have a nutritionist who suggested the formula. The base is blue-green algae, and the recipe was originally created by a doctor in Switzerland. All three of us are on the diet, in fact."

From the expression on Mom's face, Margie must have bought the story. Mom chuckled and said, "I can assure you that Deborah has a healthy appetite."

Did I ever. Even the neighbor's cat looked tasty.

"Oh, yes, we're very proud of Deborah for her loyalty. I'll tell her you said that, and I'll bring that bottle of Skin-So-Soft on Thanksgiving."

Mom looked at me seriously as she put down the receiver.

"There was a problem at school?" she asked.

I hate this about parents. How they ask a question like this when they know that there's been a problem.

"Mr. Bartlett was picking on Willy and I told him

what I thought, so he gave me detention."

"Mrs. Logan said you sacrificed yourself for Willy," Mom said, though I doubt those were Margie's actual words. "I'm very proud of you." She called to my dad, "George?"

"Hmmm?" Dad was in the den reading the news on Yahoo.

"The Logans are really nice folks. Maybe we should reconsider and eat another family."

"Eating them will be a valuable lesson for Deborah."

"Yes, dear," Mom continued, "but couldn't we cancel this once and just go hunting?"

"Deborah needs to learn our ways, now, or else . . ."

I was fed up.

"I know," I said mocking his tone of voice, "if I don't eat Willy, I'll cast shame on the family and hurt your careers."

I was madder at myself, though, for thinking of the Thanksgiving idea in the first place. I'd made a total mess out of things.

Mom stood between us in the doorway, considering what Dad had said. "I guess you're right after all, George. Margie's noticed that she doesn't eat. Perhaps Deborah's getting too close to the family."

A moment later I had a flash of inspiration.

"Mom, Dad, if Willy and his family disappear, won't there be an investigation? What if the police find out about us?"

Dad came into the room. "That's not likely to happen. The ships are close enough now to beam in cloaking devices. No one will see the Impala or us."

"Except the Logans, of course," Mom said, bursting

the rest of my bubble. "We can program their address, and if they look out the window when we drive up, no problem. I'm just amazed at the new technology."

I then had my second brilliant idea.

"They're going to tell people, you know, about how they're spending Thanksgiving and who's coming over," I said. "Humans do that sort of thing."

"Technology, darling," Mom said. "We've tapped into all their phones and computers. We're sending high-frequency amnesia pulses whenever the words *Thanksgiving* or *dinner* are mentioned."

Mom kept talking as we walked into the kitchen. "The Logans don't seem to have many close friends here in Prattville, so I don't think casual conversation will be a problem."

It went without saying that Willy wouldn't mention the get-together. What sixth-grade boy would boast he was spending Thanksgiving with a girl from his class?

All of a sudden, my tentacles popped out of my head on their own accord.

Dad winked at Mom, and he went into the living room and turned on the TV.

"Deborah, you're becoming a woman now and your emotions are fluctuating," Mom said. "This is called Disruptive Tentacle Syndrome. You'll have to wear a hat for a few months. It'll pass, but you'll need to be careful around other people."

I absolutely hated my life.

The next day I wore a dumb stocking cap to school. I endured detention with Mr. Bartlett that afternoon, and then on Monday and Tuesday. In some ways, detention was a relief because I didn't have to see Willy after school.

When he waved good-bye as he walked out the door on Tuesday, I felt my eyes sting. I squeezed them shut so I wouldn't cry. But even if they were normal salty human tears, I wouldn't have wanted Mr. Bartlett to think he'd caused them.

I suffered through the worksheets, doing stupid things like putting words into ABC order and writing math facts I knew as a two-year-old, all the while fantasizing what life might be like if I'd been put in one of the other sixth-grade classes.

As Mr. Bartlett graded papers, he mumbled to himself, more proof he was completely insane. If I ate him, would his craziness transfer to me like mad cow disease? I shuddered at the thought.

"Tony, you chump, the pyramids cannot sharpen razors," Mr. Bartlett said. "An F for you."

Mr. Bartlett was an idiot. Tony loved to make jokes, and Mr. Bartlett never got any of them. Tony had added that part sitting next to me in computer lab as we were typing our reports. He'd started laughing, and I looked over his shoulder to see what was so funny. He'd written that the pyramids were built by aliens. They were, but that's beside the point.

I waited for Mr. Bartlett to say something else sarcastic about Tony, but he'd moved on.

"Marisol Montez, are you ever going to learn that it's not House White but White House? If you can't learn the language, go back to El Salvador."

Plus, he was a creep. Marisol had been in America for less than six months. I'd like for him to write in Spanish and find out how correct his grammar was.

"Deborah . . ."

His abrasive voice made me jump. I glanced up through my bangs. He was staring at me. His eyes were unnerving, both sinister and calculating.

"What?" I asked.

"You have an exceptional ability, and I expect that you will guide our math team to victory. Do you understand?"

"I guess so," I said.

"Don't just guess. It is imperative we win."

Chill, already, I thought. Mr. Bartlett had such an ego. Room 36 *always* won the Math Champs contest, and his classes *always* had the highest scores in the school on the state tests. I was convinced that was the only reason he was allowed to keep teaching.

Then I realized why he might have been so frustrated with us. My class, in general, wasn't as strong in math as his other classes had been. His reputation was at stake.

"I expect more from you than the others," he said, "even more than from Alicia, who is quite capable, or Chen, who actually pays attention to the lessons." I didn't like how his beady little eyes kept peering into me like he was reading my mind. "Does your family have any plans for the holidays?"

Why was he being so chummy?

"Just turkey, pumpkin pie, and the Macy's Parade on TV," I lied.

"Hmmm," he said, more to himself than to me. His face hardened again. "Get back to work."

*

All Thanksgiving morning I worried. I worried so much that every hour or so *pop* went my tentacles. I had to somehow justify what we were going to do that afternoon or go crazy. Mom, Dad, and I had to eat humans to sustain us, just as a lion or a bear might eat someone they came across. People might hunt down animals, but no one would call them unethical.

My species had invaded the last planet with a decent food supply more than thirty years ago, and now almost all the food was gone. The beings there were short green froglike creatures whose passion was writing poetry. Their essences were supposedly exquisite. Mom said these frog people had supplied the invading ships and had also been sent back to the Home World because we'd eaten up almost all of the food there. But our species hadn't conserved the green frog people. Now there was no breeding stock left.

There aren't that many planets with life in our galaxy and to find one with sentient life is really difficult. As soon as the Home World honed in on Earth, my parents were sent to prepare for the next great feast.

I supposed if my species had practiced conservation we wouldn't have run out of food, and my childhood would have been totally different. But from what I knew about home, conservation wasn't one of our virtues.

One of the things we did value was a good parade. Back home we'd have one every chance we got. Dad said there's something about marching together in lockstep that makes us happy. He and I always watched the Macy's Parade on Thanksgiving. We really liked the balloons, but this year I just sat on our new beige carpet and played Solitaire, barely noticing Snoopy, or Popeye, or even Superman as they floated by.

Dad leaned back in his overstuffed chair with his feet on the ottoman and whistled "You'd Better Watch Out" along with the University of Michigan Marching Band, which was two-stepping behind Bullwinkle. A commercial came on, and I wondered vaguely what I'd get Mom and Dad for Christmas. That is, if I'd forgiven them by then.

No matter how hard I tried to justify it, I still loathed the idea of eating the Logans. We didn't have to eat *everyone* on Earth, did we? We'd have to have breeding stock, a mistake that was made with the frog people—now there was no genetic diversity and they could no longer breed.

According to Dad, there were new laws to perpetuate the food source. Dad had told me that there would even be humans whose families were exempt: certain scientists, a few artists, people with exceptional mechanical ability. "Drones," Dad called them.

Why couldn't Willy's family be drones? If Mom and Dad were going to be as high up in the government as they said they were, our family would certainly get special privileges.

I was afraid Dad might blow up at me again, but I asked him about an exemption for Willy's family anyway. Fortunately the parade had put him in a good mood.

"What do Willy's parents do for a living?"

"His dad owns a video store," I said, "and his stepmom does Web pages."

He shook his head. "Can't see how those jobs would serve the empire."

So that was that.

*

On the way to the Logans' for Thanksgiving dinner, I just stared out the car window and held the bottle of Skin-So-Soft. Dad told me to stop pouting and he and Mom chatted merrily about stupid technology the whole way there.

"Dinner will be over in a jiffy. Besides, you're a growing girl and you need to eat."

"Okay, fine," I said.

After he parked, Dad got out of the car first. Mom turned around, being careful with the pecan pie she had baked the night before.

"Your dad and I both think the world of you."

It was nice to know this, but I wondered which world they meant.

Margie evidently loved decorating for all the holidays. A wreath of crimson and gold grape leaves decorated the Logans' door. Inside, all of the coffins were closed, each draped with a festive tablecloth on which sat Hallmark figurines of Pilgrim boys and girls. I'd warned my parents about the coffins, but they still exchanged a glance. Little paper turkeys, their breasts opened in accordion pleats, hung from the ceiling in the same places the bats had been. I suspected there would be snowflakes hanging there in December.

I handed Margie the lotion as she led Mom into the kitchen. Willy grabbed Margie's dad's hand and pulled him over to me.

"Deborah, this is my new grandpa," he said. "I didn't get a chance to introduce you at the wedding."

"Nice to meet you, sir," I said, shaking his hand.

"So, you're Willy's girlfriend?" his grandfather asked.

"Grandpa!" Willy's face turned as almost as red as his hair.

On any other day I'd be mortified, but I was preoccupied, so I just smiled and kept an eye on my parents.

"There's an article about the policeman in the newspaper today, and how in the past there've been these mysterious disappearances in town," Willy said. "Usually, they were people living on the streets. Margie thinks there might be a serial killer in Prattville. Cool, huh?"

"I guess so," I said, looking over his shoulder.

"Anything wrong?" he asked.

"My dad was just lecturing me about being more responsible."

"Tell me about it. Margie got upset this morning because Dad and I forgot to buy cranberry sauce when we went to the grocery store yesterday."

I realized this was the last chance I'd have to say good-bye to Willy.

"There's something I need to tell you." I nodded for him to follow me into the dining nook because no one was there.

A burnt orange tablecloth with matching napkins covered the table. Margie had created a centerpiece with more of the colorful grape leaves, wrapping them around silver candlesticks. I picked up a fork, and found it was surprisingly heavy. The table was set with good silverware. My parents would probably want to use it.

"What's up?" he asked.

I suddenly didn't know what to say. Willy bent his head closer to me, and I squeezed the fork so hard I could feel it make an indentation into my palm. I couldn't think of anything other than how much I liked his blue eyes, red hair, and freckles.

I swallowed and got control of myself. "Thanks for being such a good friend," I said. "No matter what happens, I want you to know that."

His forehead wrinkled a bit. "What could happen?" he asked.

Just then we heard Fred call out, "Half-time's over. You want a beer, George?"

"Sure," my dad said, even though he had no intention of drinking it.

All the guys went into the den. Margie called out from the kitchen that she had to baste the turkey, but she'd be there in a jiffy. Fred turned the volume up on the TV, and sat down on the couch with his cousins. Willy plopped down in a beanbag chair, and Margie's dad settled into a recliner.

Willy crammed potato chips into his mouth and then said, "I love the Patriots."

Even talking with his mouth full, Willy was cute.

Mom, Dad, and I stood just inside the door. Everyone else had their eyes glued to the screen. To their credit, my parents were being pretty patient, considering we'd been off our schedule for three whole weeks.

The Dolphins were about to make a field goal, and my parents' tentacles rose in tandem. I guess we're pack animals. My tentacles went up, too, but once they were out of my head they hung pretty limply. The Patriots intercepted the ball, and everyone in the room let out a big cheer.

My parents stepped forward, nudging me as they did so; rows of teeth exposed one after another. I halfheartedly opened my jaws. Dad was inches away from Fred's head. He'd snap it off first. The technique was pretty bloody but effective with a large group.

Just then Dad's cell phone rang.

The three of us whipped our tentacles back inside in a microsecond. Being fast like that is an evolutionary trait. Sometimes our survival counts on it.

"Sorry about that," Dad said. He put the phone to his ear and his face turned red again. "Are you positive?"

He sounded worried. Mr. Logan clicked off the TV. The room got really quiet and everyone stared at Dad.

He hung up and put his phone back in his pocket.

"Well, uh, I'm really sorry, but it looks like we have to go."

Margie called from the kitchen.

"Is there something wrong?"

"Ah, yes," Dad said, looking at Mom, who stared at him like he'd just lost his mind. "There's been an . . . an accident . . . with our dog."

"I didn't know you had a dog," Willy said.

Dad ushered Mom and me out of the den. "We're going to have to go."

"I am so sorry," Margie said. "I'll get your coats."

When we were outside, she called after us, "Want to take the pie with you?"

"No, you enjoy it," Mom said. "Listen, I'll call you. I'd love to find out how you keep these roses blooming this late in the year."

As I buckled my seat belt, Dad put his hands on the steering wheel like he was bracing himself.

"There's a ship close enough to use cellular. It's coming in tonight north of Reno to bring in the reconnaissance team. If we leave now, we should make it before the team's sent down."

"Darling," Mom said. "I'm not going to make anything on an empty stomach."

Dad nodded. "We'll pick up something on the way."

I felt relieved. I could eat fast food with no feelings attached. That's just what I wanted.

Chapter Five

Jackpot!

Not only was the Impala invisible, with the latest work Dad had done on it, it could now fly.

"This is amazing," I said, looking down on the cars below us on the freeway.

We were heading up Interstate 80, making great time, when Dad decided to pull in at the last rest area in California before the Nevada state line.

We descended to the parking lot, and Dad turned off the engine.

"I have something to tell you, Virginia," he said after a minute or two. "When I got the call, I found out that your mother is on this team that's coming in. I was going to let you be surprised when they landed, but, knowing your mom, I decided she'd want you to be prepared."

Mom unbuckled her seat belt and planted a big kiss on Dad's cheek. She told me once that when she and Dad first got to Earth, they were appalled at the practice of kissing. Mouths back home were for eating and burping only.

The longer they lived here, though, the more they

got used to seeing people do it. One day they decided to try it and found out that, in this one matter, perhaps humans had something on us. I begged her to not go into any more details.

"Thank you, George, for telling me. Mother has always hated displays of emotion. I'll stay calm and reserved. But, oh"—Mom sort of squealed—"I'm so excited."

I frantically tried to pronounce Grandmother's name. "Pigs bucket. Pigs back." Once again, at the height of my frustration, "Pigs butt" flew out of my mouth.

Mom sighed. "It's 'Pgsbttk.' Keep practicing, dear."

"If Grandmother decides to execute me, at least I won't have to deal with not having my own room anymore," I said.

An old VW van pulled in to the parking spot next to us. I read the bumper stickers and decals that covered the van: EAT ORGANIC, NO IRRADIATED FOOD, STOP BIO-GENETIC ENGINEERING, along with FREE TIBET and THIS VAN RUNS ON BIODIESEL.

The doors opened, and several young people poured out.

Dad nodded approvingly. "College kids, more than likely, and health food store aficionados. We're in luck, no additives."

"And probably no caffeine. We might not be jittery tonight," Mom said, as we watched the group split up and disappear into the women's and men's rooms.

Mom turned a knob next to the glove compartment, and I felt the Impala emit a low-pitched vibration.

"The amnesia pulse?" I asked.

"Yes," Mom said. A car pulled out a few parking

places to the left of us. "No one will remember we've been here."

We followed the group into the bathrooms. Dad went one way, Mom and I went the other. Feeding was same-old, same-old. Just like on any Halloween, the essence fear was delicious, but we ate without the added flavor of betrayal.

When we were done, we didn't clean up every nook and cranny like we usually did. Mom considered it, but after all, we were in a bathroom, and we were on a tight schedule.

As we rose out of the parking lot, Mom pulled down her visor and switched on the little light above the mirror so she could put her lipstick back on. I asked for the floss in the glove compartment, and Dad put on an oldies station that played music from the dinosaur era. He and Mom first started to listen to radio transmissions from Earth in 1975, and I think they were imprinted. Dad turned the volume up higher and started to tap the steering wheel with his fingers.

Barry Manilow had invaded the car, and I'd left my iPod at home. There was nothing to do but endure. At least I was full, not that it helped how bad the music was.

Mom yawned and pretty soon, even with the music blasting, she was nodding off. Too much was happening for me to sleep. I was finally going to meet people from back home, Grandmother included, and I still couldn't say "Pgsbttk."

"How are they going to hide the ship?" I asked.

"It's just a small transport," Dad said. "They'll zip in and out. Earth's radar won't notice a thing because of the cloaking system. They'll beam the crew down just like in

Star Trek and then hide outside the solar system to wait for the full assault."

"Didn't the Klingons have a cloaking mechanism?" I asked.

"Yes, they had it in the second series. We developed the technology within a year after receiving the first broadcasts. For such a backward planet, Earth does have a few creative minds. You ought to see our tricorders."

"Do you think the invasion will be before Christmas?" I had another report due for Mr. Bartlett, a biography this time. If I didn't have to work on it, why bother?

Loggins and Messina were now on, and Dad tapped in time to "Your Mama Don't Dance." "Not that quickly," he said, "but by the middle of January, for sure."

January was going to be booked. My birthday was on the fourteenth. Math Champs was scheduled for the seventeeth. I told Dad that it would be nice if the invasion could happen afterward. He agreed, but then he said, "Maybe you'll be showing off your math skills for Our Most Supreme Imperial High Matriarch instead."

An incredibly long commercial for Carpet King came on. Dad tuned the radio to a station broadcasting in Spanish, and below us we saw the lights of several emergency vehicles heading west on the other side of the freeway. Did we forget to eat a body part or something? I felt a twinge of nervousness, but Dad acted like he didn't even notice.

When we crossed the state line, we were almost out of gas. Dad landed the Impala on a deserted frontage road and turned off the cloaking device. We got back on the freeway, and he drove into Reno.

When he pulled off the road, Mom woke up. She and

I walked inside the mini-mart to stretch our legs while he was at the gas pump.

I wandered off to the magazine rack.

"You go on, dear," Mom said to me as she turned toward a trail of tinny music to the row of slot machines. "I feel lucky tonight."

"Do you think you should, Mom?"

Mom had a bit of a gambling problem. The last time Mom and Dad went to Reno, she couldn't pull herself away from the slots. For hours, Mom walked up and down the aisles of the casinos and scanned the machines. Based on the sequence of Jacks, four-leaf clovers, and horseshoes that showed up on the display, she could calculate how soon a machine would have a jackpot, down to how many quarters she'd have to play to get it. Dad had a heck of a time getting her out of there.

Mom also had another edge. Our bodies emit a magnetic field that can affect machines if we focus on them. Mom easily manipulated slot machines with her field to help with the possibility of a jackpot.

Dad was worried she might have a problem, and that her incredible luck—that is, her skills in probability (females of our species especially have exceptional math skills), plus her use of her magnetic field—would make the authorities suspicious. Mom told Dad he was being a worrywart; somebody had to win, so why not her?

"Dad's not going to like this," I warned Mom.

"Oh, there's nothing wrong with having a little fun," she told me and walked over to the first machine. She touched its shiny metal surface like it was a brand-new car.

In less than a minute, I heard a bunch of bells and

wild music playing. *Oh, brother,* I thought. Sure enough, lights were flashing when I turned around, and Mom was jumping up and down clapping her hands. Quarters poured from the slot machine like a silver waterfall.

The clerk whipped out his camera and took a Polaroid of Mom. He fanned the print while she scooped the money into her purse.

"Oh, can you believe it?" she shouted.

I ran over and helped her with the coins.

"Mom, you've won a hundred dollars."

She whispered so the clerk couldn't hear. "The array on the machine was perfect."

Her purse was bulging by then. The clerk brought over two buckets that said I ♥ RENO. I wanted to get out of there before Dad came in, so I started shoveling quarters into them as fast as I could.

But not fast enough. When Dad walked into the store and saw what was happening, his hat shifted a quarter turn. He reached up and yanked it back around.

"We have to go *now*."

Mom grabbed a last handful of quarters.

The clerk had taped her picture next to ten or twelve photos of other lucky winners. Dad strode over, grabbed it from the window, and tore it up.

"You're such a party pooper, dear," Mom said as he marched her back to the car.

Mom put the buckets in the backseat with me. As Dad turned on the engine, he said to Mom, "We're supposed to keep a low profile, tonight of all nights."

The excitement drained from Mom's face and she looked like she was about to cry. "But the money will pay for our trip."

Dad shook his head and didn't say anything else for the next several miles. I wasn't worried, though. He could never stay mad at Mom for very long. We drove through town and then turned north. Pretty soon there was just sagebrush on either side of the road. I peered up at the sky to see if there was any sign of the ship.

"Just think of it," Dad said, patting Mom's hand now, "by this time next year, duty and career will have met. We could be sitting on the Supreme High Council."

Mom sighed. "We deserve it. We've certainly paid our dues."

"Me, too," I said from the backseat. "I'm the one who'll be sleeping on the couch."

I wondered if my grandmother would appreciate the periwinkle flower pattern on my sheets. I'd just changed them that morning.

Dad's phone rang and a three-dimensional map rose out of the ashtray.

"Wow," I said.

"I configured that last week. I guess I forgot to tell you," Mom whispered, and then she put her finger to her lips. "We need to concentrate now. Remember what we taught you."

So this was finally it. Dad turned up a dirt road. We bumped along, all of our tentacles extended, the little hairs on them vibrating with ultrasonic frequency. Dad rolled back the roof so we could pick up the signal better. A blast of freezing air rushed into the car.

I had to admit that I was getting into the experience. For the very first time, I picked up on the unique genetic signature that could only come from my own species. It transmitted into my tentacles, little beeps and buzzes not too different from Morse Code. A surge of homesickness came over me for a planet I'd never seen.

I wanted to tell Willy about all of this.

But I couldn't tell him, anything. I had to make up a story about a dumb dog by next Monday.

A bright light flashed across the windshield. I blinked, just as a huge *whooshing* sound came out of the sky, like a fifty-foot tennis racket swinging through the air.

The light divided into three separate silver beams, and our car heated like an oven. Dad slammed on the brakes and we fishtailed in the sand. I heard three thuds outside the car.

Two men in silver jumpsuits surrounded by a cloud of dust stood right in front of where our car was headed. They raised their hands and screamed what must have been the Home World equivalent of "Stop!"

Dad slammed on the brakes, and several quarters from the buckets next to me on the floorboard sloshed over my feet. The car stopped just in time. We all took a deep breath and then jumped out to see if everyone was all right.

Mom walked over to the elder of the two men and offered her hand.

"So nice to meet you," she said. She turned then to the younger man. "And Grlplktf, you've grown up! I didn't know you were coming."

The younger man blushed, while the other just stared at her.

"Pardon my manners," she said, and then spat on both of her palms and held them up to them. They each spat on one of theirs and placed them palm to palm with hers.

Customs from home were so gross.

Behind us, Dad was trying to dust off an older female.

"*Bzkrg flgngkp fl. Rhvqqtglf, hnjjjjflk,*" she told Dad, slapping his hand away.

His coordinates were a half meter off, she was saying, and she thought this was pretty sloppy work on his part.

"Well, we don't get to do this much," Dad said. "We're a little rusty."

"Mother!" Mom shouted, running past me with out-flung arms, forgetting her earlier promise of reserve. "I can't believe you're here!"

My grandmother stood rigid, not returning the hug, until my mother forced her arms down and spat on her palms again.

There were no smiles from Grandmother as she returned the greeting.

Mom tried to cover her blunder by saying, "George, Grlplktf is here, too. Isn't that nice?"

"Virginia, remember, please call him Gerald," Dad said. "That's his Earth name now."

Mom was so nervous, I felt sorry for her. I was feeling pretty sorry for myself, as well. *Pig's Butt, Pig's Butt, Pig's Butt* echoed through my head.

Mom yanked me by the arm so I stood next to her. "Mother, this is your granddaughter, Dbkrrrsh."

Grandmother had steel gray hair cut short in a no-nonsense, almost masculine way. A few wrinkles crossed her face like scars, but she was lean and looked fitter than either of my parents. I bet she worked out.

Mom nudged me, and I remembered to bow.

"*Flmxflkdbrg clclsssspd hm rwzkpp,*" Grandmother said.

That's an idiom, and hard to translate, but it roughly means: "May you suck the marrow from the bones of your enemies."

I looked at the toes of my sneakers. It would be bad manners if I straightened before I answered her. I said the one thing that I knew I could pronounce, "*Vlkm d trn,*" "Welcome to Earth," and then, because etiquette demanded I say her name, I took a big breath and said, "P . . . P . . . P . . . Pgsbttk."

I said her name perfectly, and Mom and Dad let out sighs of relief.

"Stand up." Grandmother's voice reminded me of Mr. Bartlett telling us to get ready for the Pledge of Allegiance.

I followed her order. Grandmother Pig's Butt spat on her palm, looking at me like I was an ant ready to be sacrificed for the good of the colony. I copied and held my hand out to her.

We touched, and I felt a slight tingling go up my arm. I hadn't known saliva could conduct electrical impulses between bodies. I still thought the custom was disgusting.

When we were finished, Grandmother looked around at the rest of the group. Her expression didn't change in the least. "Let's conquer this planet," she barked.

From what Mom had said, I knew not to expect a cuddly grandma who'd get all gooey over me. But here I was, her only grandchild, and after this initial spit and greet she acted like I wasn't there.

We'd had a box in the trunk of the car for years, and I always wondered what was in it. I thought maybe some sort of secret weapons, but when my dad opened it there was just a bunch of clothes from the thrift shop. I was disappointed, but I had to hand it to my parents. They planned even small details like this, which was what made them so good at their jobs.

The Home World defied fashion. Everyone wore the same silver bodysuit from cradle to grave. If our three new guests had worn theirs into Reno, people might have thought they were a trapeze act at Circus-Circus, except that on the back of each was an emblem depicting a feeding party. All the tentacles and blood might have caused some concern.

Grandmother chose a lavender pantsuit. The other two put on flannel shirts, jeans, and boots. All they needed was suspenders to look like lumberjacks.

As we turned back toward Reno on the highway, Grandmother complained, "This is a very primitive mode of transportation."

She was sitting between my parents in the bench seat in front. Her Earth name was going to be Peggy. Stan and Gerald were in back with me.

Stan smiled and asked, "Casino?"

Gerald had the same type of goofy grin. "Lucky Nugget?"

Hearing this, Grandmother announced, "I booked rooms for all of us. I put them on your credit card."

Dad glanced over to Mom. "You gave them our credit card number?"

"Don't worry. I had a secure connection with the ship's computer." Mom turned to Grandmother. "No one on the ship told me you were coming."

Grandmother ignored her. "We also charged a Hummer. We can pick it up in Reno.

"No money down," Stan and Gerald chanted together. "Zero percent financing, and no payments for the first three months."

"They've been learning English off the satellites," Grandmother said. "Give them a few days, and they'll pick up the rest of the language."

Dad was having a hard time not blowing his top. "Look, Peggy," he said, calling her by her Earth name. "We're having a hard enough time just meeting our mortgage."

I think he was exaggerating a bit. We're not exactly flush, but we do okay.

"It's apparent you've been corrupted by the materialistic values of this society," Grandmother said.

Maybe Mom could warm Grandmother up with some free Avon samples, but from what I could tell about her, I doubted she'd want any *Skin-So-Soft*.

Stan and Gerald started to sing the jingle in the commercials for the Lucky Nugget. I rolled up my jacket for a pillow. Leaning my head against the window, the last thing I heard was Mom telling Dad, "Don't worry, honey. I'm sure we'll invade long before the next bill comes due."

Chapter Six

Cruising the Casino

By the time we got to the Lucky Nugget, I was so sleepy I hardly remembered Dad checking us in. When I woke up the next morning, he was snoring in the other bed. Mom must have gotten up early because she wasn't there. Grandmother and the others must have slept in another room. I turned on the TV low enough not to wake up Dad. I watched cartoons for a while and then changed the station.

There was a group of newspaper reporters standing outside the Lucky Nugget's lobby interviewing a large man in a suit. The caption on the bottom of the screen said he was the chief of police.

Uh-oh, I thought.

"The second incident happened here approximately seven hours after the slayings in the rest area in California," he was saying. I'd been right. We'd been too careless at the rest stop. "The other evidence found early this morning in the third-floor linen closet of the Lucky Nugget seems to indicate the killer struck again at approximately two A.M."

The reporters started to ask questions at the same time, but the chief refused to answer any of them. Just then Mom burst into the room carrying all sorts of packages. Grandmother and the lumberjacks followed her. Dad sat up and yawned.

"We've had so much fun," Mom said. "I made a killing at the craps table last night."

Grandmother zeroed in on the television. The police chief was saying that the casino was going to be searched top to bottom and that none of the guests would be allowed to leave until further notice. She glared at Stan and Gerald with her tentacles fully raised, and I thought for a moment that she might eat the two of them then and there. There were stories of that sort of thing happening.

"*Flmxshpld blkvvgrnd flkl bfklk rmpldm? Czhfmdb bkplwnl tw d vbz?*"

Which translates as: "Which of you two brainless dolts couldn't wait to feed? Or was it both of you?"

Stan and Gerald looked down at the floor. "Three obese tourists from Minnesota and a woman pushing a cart with bathroom supplies," Stan said.

"We were so hungry, but they were quite filling," Gerald said.

"I told you to wait until the time was safe," Grandmother scolded. "The Supreme High Council will hear of this."

Dad was sitting on the bed with his head in his hands. "All my hard work," he was saying. "All the years of planning."

Grandmother walked over to him and smacked him with her purse. "And this is for choosing to feed in a public location and leaving evidence. *Flplk*."

(If I translated *flplk*, you wouldn't be allowed to read this book.)

"Mother," Mom said. "If you're going to insult my husband, then you can just . . . just go back home. We were desperately hungry. The Impala was cloaked. No one saw us. There's no way they could track us down."

"They were organic," I added, trying to help, "and good for us."

Everyone ignored me, of course.

"We all know that returning without accomplishing our mission is impossible," Grandmother said. "I'm going to my room. I need to rest and calculate a way to clean up this situation. Chances are the resistance will hear of this and be on alert."

"I thought you said there wasn't any resistance," I said to Mom as Grandmother slammed the door.

"There isn't, Deborah, but Mother is old school, and you can't convince her of anything," Mom said. "Oh, I always hated it when she got angry like this back home."

Stan, still looking guilty, said, "We're going to play keno," and pulled Gerald by the arm out of the room.

"Do you think Gerald will get carded?" I asked.

"I give up," Dad said, and went into the bathroom.

"George didn't say a word about my good luck," Mom said, and yawned. We heard the shower turn on. "Your father needs to learn to have a little fun. I'm sure things will work out. They always do."

Mom was asleep by the time Dad got out of the bathroom. He was in a better mood. He put his shoes on by the side of the bed and then leaned over to kiss her.

"I love the little sounds she makes when she sleeps,"

he told me. "Just like a Pekingese snoring. Well, kid, since we're stuck, want to explore the place?"

Dad and I took the elevator downstairs. We skirted the edges of the casino since I wasn't allowed in, but the beeping and buzzing and loopy music were still pretty noisy. There was a line of people waiting for a breakfast buffet on the other side of the room. I pulled Dad over and looked through the window.

There were piles of fruit and pastries and pans of eggs, sausage, and potatoes. The human diet has so much more variety than ours. For us, it's just protein, fat, and calcium, along with the extra fiber provided by clothes. I loved the aroma of Earth food. I wished I could eat like a normal human girl and drink sodas and milk shakes and find out what pizza tasted like.

My ski cap began to rise.

Dad put his hand on top of my head and gently pushed my tentacles back down. "Deborah, sometimes I'd really like to put my lips around a big prime rib. A nice rare one."

"Do you think human food would really kill us?" I asked, embarrassed about my lack of tentacle control.

"We can't take the chance of finding out," he said.

All the noise was beginning to get on my nerves, so we walked to the hotel lobby.

"Look, Dad." There was a life-size cutout of Jimmy Joe Crawford, my mom's favorite country singer. I was so tired the night before, I'd missed it. "He's playing here tonight. This is his last tour, you know. Mom says he's tired of traveling."

Dad smiled. "Want to surprise her?"

Dad got tickets for the two of them. Since I was

underage, I had to hang out with Grandmother and the boys for the evening.

Mom was beside herself when Dad gave her the tickets. I hadn't seen her so happy since . . . well, ever. Dad kept a close watch on her for the rest of the day. I saw her glance sideways at the slot machines once or twice when we passed by, but she didn't complain.

Stan, Gerald, Grandmother, and I went to an arcade during the Jimmy Joe Crawford show with a bucket of the quarters Mom had won at the gas station. I didn't have to teach them how to play any of the games. It's amazing what the ships could upload from Earth.

Grandmother liked the ones with guns best and blew away about a hundred terrorists in Xtrm Combat. A crowd started to gather to watch this little old lady in a lavender pantsuit whoop it up each time she blasted another man with a black mask over his head. Stan and Gerald weren't having much luck, though. I think Gerald said "This sucks" in Lithuanian.

"Did you get Lithuanian TV channels on the ships, too?" I asked.

"We had language tapes for it," Gerald said. "We are visitors from Lithuania. That is our camouflage."

I was confused for a moment, and then I figured out what he was trying to say. "You mean your cover? You're pretending to be from Lithuania?"

Stan nodded enthusiastically. "We study only a little bit of English, so not knowing it so good would make us seem more . . ." He hunted for the right word.

"Foreign?" I said for him. "I'm impressed with how much you've picked up in less than twenty-four hours."

The three of us sat at a table near Grandmother's Xtrm Combat machine.

"So, what's it like back home?" I asked.

They looked at me strangely for a moment, but then Stan's face lit up.

"I understand," he said. Then just as quickly he frowned. "Not so good. Very little food left on sensitive frog planet, but we will conquer this one and have fresh new food source."

"I guess you could look at it that way, but I know a lot of nice people here," I said. "Dad says I've got to be tough, but I'm really not looking forward to seeing them get eaten." I played with a ring tab from a soda can that had been left on the table. "I guess it was a long time since you fed? Since you ate those people last night so fast and all."

Gerald hung his head. "Couldn't help ourselves."

"Believe me, I know what that's like." I said. "What about Grandmother?"

Stan sighed. "We don't know how she holds out."

Gerald seemed to be the shyer of the two. He gave me a little smile, like he knew something I didn't. I smiled back just to be polite. Too bad acne was a universal problem. Kids have it back home, too, and it seemed to have extruded through his human overskin. He might have been cute, otherwise.

"You two will make a very nice couple," Stan said.

"Excuse me?" I asked.

Gerald's face turned pink beneath his pimples.

"You don't know?" Stan said, looking embarrassed. "You're betrothed. The two of you. Happy ever after. Marital bliss ahead in the future."

Gerald was the boy from home I was supposed to marry?

Before I could say anything, Grandmother walked over. Her fans gave her a round of applause for her performance. One guy called out, "Way to go, Granny." She ignored him.

"Your parents should be finished with their hedonistic pastime."

"You were having fun," I said. I felt I had to defend Mom and Dad, even if they had arranged my engagement with a total stranger.

"I never *just* have fun," she said.

"Peggy excels with all types of weapons," Stan said.

Was he kissing up to her? Since they didn't kiss on the Home World, maybe the expression would be "*spitting up to her*"?

"I thought it would be good to practice with typical Earth weapons, even if they were just prototypes," she said.

Geez, even if Stan was just trying to get on her good side, she could at least say "Thank you." Was this woman ever pleasant?

"Mom must have taken after Grandfather." The words slipped out of my mouth before I had a chance to stop them.

"Unfortunately, yes," Grandmother agreed.

Make a note of it, I thought. *No sense of humor.*

The four of us walked to the theater just as the early show was letting out. Mom saw us and ran over.

"We were in the front row, can you believe that?" she said. "Jimmy Joe blew a kiss toward me."

"Where's Dad?" I asked.

"He was right behind me," Mom said, looking around.

Dad walked out of the theater with his hands in his pockets. "I got a little present for you," he said when he reached Mom. He whipped out a napkin. TO VIRGINIA, LOVE FROM JIMMY JOE CRAWFORD was written across it in hot pink ink.

"How did you manage?" Mom asked Dad, and then, holding the napkin to her heart, she leaned over and kissed him.

Grandmother, Stan, and Gerald sucked in their breath with shock. "Disgusting," they all said at once.

Would I ever want to kiss Gerald? The invasion was really going to happen, but was I really engaged to him? I made a face that matched the others.

"Disgusting," I whispered to myself.

"Mom, Dad, there's something I've got to talk to you about," I said, "in private."

At least puberty had one thing going for it. The word "private" had a lot more power than it used to.

"We'll meet you and the boys in your room in a few minutes," Mom told Grandmother.

"Be quick," Grandmother said, and did an about-face like she'd been in the military.

"What's this about Gerald and me?" I asked.

Mom's hand went to her mouth, and she cast a side-ward glance at Dad. "We were going to tell you, Deborah," she said. "Honestly, as soon as we got home. Your *clmcht* with Gerald happened when you were a baby."

"My what?"

"Your betrothal," Dad explained. "Gerald and you both belong to the House of Mpfld."

"But if we belong to the same house, that means Gerald's my cousin. Mom, Dad, please don't make me do this."

Both of my parents reached for my head. Mom's hand got there first, popping my tentacles back down.

Mom frowned. "Grlplktf is your *distant* cousin, so far back that it won't matter for your breeding."

"Oh, god, Mother. Yuck."

"You'll feel differently about him someday," Mom said, and then she leaned over to whisper in my ear. "You will not refuse to marry him when the time comes, do you understand? Your father's career is at stake. And so is mine, and I'm not talking about Avon. If you disgrace us by complaining about your betrothal, Mother will report it, and your future, young lady, will be over."

We made our way to Grandmother's room. I sulked while the rest talked about what to do if we weren't able to leave the hotel by the next morning. The ship that dropped off the team was well beyond Neptune by now and couldn't beam us anywhere. We'd just started to make a list of strategies when there was a knock at the door.

"Sorry to bother you folks," a woman said. She held up a badge. "I'm Susan Mackenzie, FBI. This is my partner, Ed Samuelson." The two of them squeezed into the room past Grandmother. "I apologize for it being so late, but we need to interview everyone at the hotel." She counted us and then looked at a list of names on a clipboard. "You're the Jones family? The six of you checked in a few hours before the murders. Did you see anything you might consider unusual last night?"

Oh, no, nothing much, I thought. *Just the usual inter-galactic drop-off.*

"We also need a sample of your DNA," she said. This was bad news for us, but I couldn't help thinking that I liked her haircut. She had short blond wavy hair, one side a little longer than the other. I wondered if Mom would let me have a perm when we got back home. "We're taking some from everybody," she continued. "Just a swab inside your cheek. Who'd like to go first?"

I felt the grown-ups freeze. Any pathologist would know that she had run across something very, very strange. It wouldn't take long for a lab to determine our DNA samples didn't come from anything known on Earth.

Grandmother stepped up to the two agents. I knew she hadn't eaten, so I closed my eyes and waited to hear the first sounds of ripping flesh.

Chapter Seven

Mom Loses It

I expected carnage, but instead Grandmother started talking in Lithuanian. Both of the agents looked at her slack jawed, and I could almost hear them think, "Huh?"

"These are my wife's relatives visiting from Europe," Dad said. His forehead was beaded with sweat.

Mom said something in Lithuanian, and Stan and Gerald whipped passports out of their pockets. The other agent inspected them, and then Grandmother handed hers over to Agent Mackenzie. A fine powder floated up from the pages like pollen coming off a flower. The two agents both sneezed and then stood at attention with blank eyes.

Mother reached into her purse. She pulled out several vials, some marked with an X, the others with a Y. Each contained a cotton swab.

"I never go anywhere without these ever since all those crime shows have been on TV," she said, while the agents stared unblinkingly. "I've been taking DNA samples from all my Avon customers, the men and the women." She turned to Grandmother. "I bet you don't know how many men purchase cosmetics these days." Grandmother looked incredulous. "I've been telling them I'm collecting samples for antiaging research that the company's doing."

Mom read several labels on the swabs and then handed them to Agent Mackenzie. "Agent Mackenzie," she said softly, "I want you to do something for me."

The agent's eyes fluttered a bit. Mom whispered our Earth names into her ears, and, like a puppet, Agent Mackenzie wrote each of them on the vials that Mom had brought and put the swabs into her evidence box.

"That's it," Mom said when she was done.

Grandmother walked over to Agent Samuelson and snapped her fingers in front of his face. When he didn't respond, she said, "We have a couple of minutes before the effects wear off."

I watched the teamwork between Mom and Grandmother and wondered if someday in the future Mom and I'd be working together.

"I suppose your time here on Earth hasn't been totally useless," Grandmother said.

I didn't think what Grandmother said was much of a compliment, but Mom stood up a little straighter.

Dad pulled back the curtain and looked out the window at the parking lot. Mom unfolded her napkin and studied Jimmy Joe's signature with a funny smile on her face. Stan lay down on the bed with his shoes on, humming the Lucky Nugget jingle. I caught Gerald looking at me, and he blushed again.

At the same moment, the bodies of the two agents

became less rigid, and they both yawned simultaneously.

"Ah, yes," Agent Mackenzie said. "Thank you. You can enjoy the casino and the other facilities, but you cannot leave the premises. All of the exits are guarded."

The two of them walked out of the room.

"Glad that's over," Mom said. A big smile crossed her face. "I know what I want to do. Which way to the poker tables?"

Mom wasn't in the room when we woke up the next morning. Dad called Grandmother's room and she wasn't there either. We met Grandmother at the elevator door, and the three of us went down to the casino.

We finally found Mom on a bench in front of the restaurant with the great breakfast buffet. Her mascara was smeared and she grasped a tissue, hiding the red stains from her tears. Agent Mackenzie was kneeling next to her, holding her other hand. Mom turned her head away when we came up to her.

"What are you doing with her?" Grandmother asked the agent, not sounding anything like a Lithuanian.

Grandmother evidently didn't realize that on Earth, if someone was as upset as Mom, normal behavior would be to try to comfort her, instead of asking rude questions of a person who appeared to be helping.

Dad shot Grandmother a quick glance that said more or less, "Cool your jets, Granny."

Agent Mackenzie wore a baby blue turtleneck top with a smartly cut jacket that was just a shade darker and a pair of black slacks. She looked as though she was dressed to play the part of an FBI agent in a movie.

She regarded Grandmother with a cool expression.

You could see she was used to working with difficult people and wasn't intimidated in the least.

"I was on my way to breakfast, and I saw Mrs. Jones sitting here. Something was wrong, so I thought I'd see if I could help."

That sounded logical to me, but I sensed Grandmother was still suspicious.

"I lost everything," Mom said. "Even the extra cash we took out of the ATM before we left Prattville. And I'm afraid I put a cash advance on the credit card." Dad didn't say a word, and his hat stayed level on his head. Even still, I could tell he was fuming. "It won't happen again, George, I promise."

All of a sudden all the trilling and *ding ding-a-ling*-ings of the slot machines stopped.

"Attention, guests. Attention. You are now free to leave the casino. We're sorry for any inconvenience and hope you come back soon. Remember, you're always a winner at the Lucky Nugget."

Quicker than a flash of neon, the racket was back on.

"Let's get out of here," Dad said, looking nervously at Agent Mackenzie.

"We've been talking about getting help," the agent said. "I hope Virginia follows up on it."

"You've been very kind," Mom told Agent Mackenzie.

"It's the least I could do," she said. Nodding to the rest of us, she proceeded into the restaurant.

Dad was flustered. "Let's get out of here," he said again. "Now."

We found Stan and Gerald playing keno, and the six of us went up to our rooms to get our things.

"I don't know what happened," Mom said in the

74

elevator. "Probability was on my side. I kept playing and playing, counting cards, thinking I had to win, but the man sitting next to me got the ace of diamonds I was sure belonged to me. Oh, George"—Mom grabbed hold of Dad's arm—"I should have stuck with slot machines, but I wanted to experience the thrill of a real poker game."

"Never bet against the house," Grandmother said. I wondered where she'd picked up that expression. "And I wouldn't bet against that agent. She makes me uneasy. If I hadn't just landed on Earth, I'd say I knew her from somewhere."

"We could eat her," Stan suggested.

"We might as well eat the entire department of Homeland Security," Dad said just before the elevator door opened. "Forget it."

Within twenty minutes we were cruising through Reno on our way to get Grandmother's Hummer. No one said much, except for Stan and Gerald, who kept pointing to places like Burger King and Kentucky Fried Chicken, saying, "Ooooooh!"

"We plan to convert restaurants and have franchises," Gerald said.

"Would it be profitable?" I asked. "I mean, we don't eat that often."

"There have been recent studies done that suggest it may be healthier for us to eat more frequently but in smaller quantities," Grandmother said, rolling down the window and sniffing Earth's atmosphere. "A lot of thought has been put into this invasion. We're going to make Earth's resources last for us and not deplete them."

"That's quite a change of policy," Mom said.

We finally arrived at the car dealership. Mom pulled out a fake driver's license for Grandmother, and pretty soon the Hummer was all hers.

"I thought they weren't going to deplete the resources," I whispered to Mom.

She was checking out the retractable cup holder and shushed me. "Not *all* of them, dear."

Grandmother and the lumberjacks climbed into the Hummer.

"We'll be back in a week or so," Grandmother said, pulling a pocket road atlas out of her purse.

"You're not coming home with us?" Mom asked.

Grandmother pointed to an isolated area in southern Nevada. "Our destination is here. From your reports, this is the area that most closely resembles the Home World to prepare for the—" She stopped in mid-sentence.

Both of my parents gave me a dopey look and sighed.

"Prepare for what?" I asked.

The only answer I got was Stan revving the motor. He'd put on some reflective shades and a baseball cap. "*Hasta la vista*," he said, and the three of them pulled out. Only Gerald waved good-bye.

"Prepare for what?" I asked my parents again. "Don't tell me it's the wedding."

"No, not the wedding," Dad said. "That's not for at least another year."

They both clammed up. I wasn't going to get an answer.

On our way back to Prattville, the ramp leading to the rest area where we'd dined was closed. Snowflakes were beginning to fall.

"We don't have anything to worry about, do we?" I asked.

"Of course, not, dear," Mom said, biting her nails.

Dad's hat wobbled a bit. I hoped Mom was right.

Even though we'd just been gone a couple of days, so much had happened that it seemed like an eternity since I'd seen Willy. Our answering machine was blinking when we walked into the house, and I hoped it was a message from him.

The call was from Margie, instead. "Hey, just calling to find out how your dog is doing. I hope everything is all right. Give us a call."

Dad grumbled, wondering what she was talking about, and I had to remind him what he'd told the Logans at Thanksgiving before we made our exit.

I called Willy right away.

"Our dog didn't make it," I said in a sad voice.

"I'm really sorry," he said. "When did you get it?"

"Just the other day from the pound," I said, crossing my fingers for the second time that day.

"I think I can cheer you up," Willy said. "It's started to snow in the mountains. The weather report says a foot and a half is expected tonight."

"Yeah?" I said. We'd seen the first flakes begin to fall on our way down from Reno.

"Do you think your parents would let you go snowboarding next Saturday?"

"I've never even skied before," I said. "I'm not sure they'll let me."

"You've got to talk them into it," Willy said. "There's nothing like snowboarding. I can teach you everything about it."

I hung up, and for the first time in a long time I wasn't thinking about feeding or invasions or strange relatives from outer space. All I wanted to do was have fun.

When I returned to school after Thanksgiving vacation, Mr. Bartlett didn't tempt me at all, now that my stomachs were full. This didn't make me like him any better, though.

Chen, Alicia, and I sat at our station at the back table. Mr. Bartlett was hovering over Willy, who was so nervous that he'd snapped the points of all the pencils he had in his desk.

"You've broken your pencils on purpose," Mr. Bartlett said. "Write with a crayon."

"Oh, brother," Chen said next to me. "I can't wait until vacation."

Chen was usually pretty quiet, but when he did have something to say, he got to the point. Since finding out that the invasion was coming to pass, I'd started to put kids in my class into two categories. Alicia was definitely on the "meat" side. Chen was on my "vegetable" list, a kid I hoped would somehow survive.

Alicia opened the folder that Mr. Bartlett had prepared for us today and glanced at our instructions.

"Probability," she moaned.

After what happened in Reno with my mom, probability wasn't my favorite part of math, either. I looked over the problem Mr. Bartlett had given us.

From right to left on the number line, order the events based on how likely they are to occur.

    a. The event is certain to happen.
    b. The event is just as likely to happen as not to happen.
    c. The event has no chance of happening.
    d. The event could happen but is unlikely.
    e. The event is likely to happen.

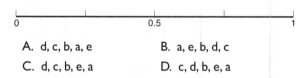

    A. d, c, b, a, e   B. a, e, b, d, c
    C. d, c, b, e, a   D. c, d, b, e, a

Easy peasy. I knew the answer immediately: D.

It took the other two half an hour to figure it out. Humans!

I asked Dad about the snowboarding trip right after the *Nightly Business Report* was over. The stock market went way up, and he was in a good mood. But just as I anticipated, Dad hated the idea.

"You could get hurt and need X-rays," Dad told me. "And then what will we do when they see you're not human?"

"I promise I'll be safe," I reasoned. When that didn't work, I asked, "Didn't you want to do fun things with your friends when you were a kid?" Finally, I said,

"Besides, I could teach the others how to snowboard if I get good at it."

"You know, George," Mom said, looking up from her Avon order, "that might help our standing with the Supreme High Council. They're always looking for new things to do with their families."

Dad thought for a moment, and then said, "You know, you might be right. They've been cooped up aboard ship for a long time. After they feed, the Council probably will want to have some fun. We might be remembered as the family who has the inside scoop on planet Earth. It couldn't hurt when they're considering new members."

I threw my arms around his neck and released all my tentacles to hug him with, too. "Thanks, Dad," I said. "Thanks so much. I can't wait to tell Willy."

"I guess I'll get to work making more of those disgusting green wafers," Mom said. "George, you're going to have to choke some down in front of the Logans."

When I got home from school the next day, there was a brand-new snowboard sitting on the kitchen table.

"We decided to give you your Christmas present early," Dad said.

I was going on a vacation, just like a real human kid!

Chapter Eight

Alley-Oops

I'd lived in the Sacramento Valley since I was three months old, and though we were close to the Sierras, we'd never gone to the snow. Now, for the second time in two weeks, Dad and I were headed up I-80, this time to Sky Ridge Ski Resort.

In the past my parents shook their heads at news stories about bumper-to-bumper traffic jams in the blizzards, wondering why humans wanted to torture themselves so much. They didn't understand that the fun you might have at the ski resorts might be worth all the hassle of getting there.

We were lucky, though. The storm had lasted until Thursday night and dumped even more snow than the weather report had predicted, but by Saturday the sky was crystal blue and the road was clear.

We met Willy's family in the lodge. In no time Willy and I were on a bunny hill for boarders. He helped me snap my feet to the board and showed me how to keep my balance while squatting as low as I could. He said he was learning to bone, to straighten his legs all the way out on certain parts of the ride, down the bigger hills.

I got the hang of snowboarding really fast. After two runs down the hill, I told Willy I was ready for the more advanced slopes.

"You're sure?" he asked. "I don't want you to get hurt."

"I'll be fine," I said.

"I stayed on this hill all day the first time I came here. Took me that long to learn to find my balance."

Willy wasn't a star at P.E., either.

"I'm ready," I declared.

He smiled. "Okay, I'm kind of bored with this anyway."

We took a lift to freeride down a fairly steep slope.

"The trial is going to start next week," Willy said.

"What trial?" I asked.

Willy looked at me blankly for a moment, as though he couldn't believe I'd forgotten about something of such importance to him.

"The ACLU, remember?" he finally asked. "My right to celebrate the month of Halloween the way my family sees fit. My right to dress like a vampire."

"Oh, sorry," I said. So much had happened between Halloween and now, I'd completely forgotten about the trial. "So, how's it going?"

"Dad and Margie act like my whole future depends on us winning, but I'm scared we'll lose. Do you think we have a chance, Deborah?"

"Sure you do," I told him.

I looked down through my feet and saw someone

leap off a huge rock buried by the snow.

"Look at that," I said.

The boarder landed beautifully. Another one followed right behind and crashed. His body spun in circles until he was too far in back of us to see any longer.

"What do you think will happen at the trial?" Willy asked again at the top.

"Uh, I don't know," I said. "I'm sure it will work out. For now, let's just enjoy the slopes. See you down below!"

I snapped in my back foot and pushed off.

I loved how the cold bored into my nostrils together with the slightly tart smell of the snow. I loved how my cheeks burned and the squishy sounds our snow boots made. I loved the smooth sliding of the board. What I loved the most, though, was going fast.

I thought I heard Willy yelling from somewhere behind me, "Don't!" but the word just whooshed past my ear.

The board skimmed over the snow. Now the snow was less deep and the tone of the ride changed. I crouched lower and sailed into the air. This was what Mom must have meant about how weightlessness in space was divine. I was lighter than air. I was a bird gliding back to earth. I made a perfect landing.

I heard Willy scream behind me. I slowed to a stop, turned around, and saw him rolling in the snow beneath the rock.

"Are you all right?" I shouted when he came to a stop.

"Yeah," he said, pulling himself slowly out from under the small avalanche he'd caused.

"Are you sure?"

"I'm fine," he said testily. "I'll catch up with you."

"If you say so," I said.

I pushed off again. My feet seemed to be talking to the board, and I let it take me to the bottom of the hill. I waited for Willy there. He'd fallen again and looked like an eleven-year-old abominable snowman by the time he got to me.

"You've really never snowboarded before?" he asked.

I shook my head. "Want to go down again?"

"No," he said, with a little too much emphasis. "Let's try the half-pipe."

We went back up the lift, and I followed Willy down to something else. Snowboarders were riding up and down the sides doing tricks.

"See how she catches air?" Willy asked, pointing to a girl who looked about seventeen. She turned around so she was facing the opposite direction. "That's called an alley-oop. I've been trying to do that for over a year."

I watched as she spun halfway around again and calculated the speed that she needed to pull off the move. I made a note of how the angle of her body intersected with the slope of the half-pipe.

"You want to try?" Willy asked.

"Okay."

Willy climbed right on the pipe and began to ride from one side to the other. He picked up speed, going higher and higher. His form wasn't that bad, but he needed to loosen up. He kept his body too tense. He tried one alley-oop after another, but he just couldn't get the hang of it. He finally crashed into another boarder, and they tumbled to the bottom.

I knew I could do any trick the other boarders were

doing, but I held back because I didn't want Willy to think I was trying to compete with him. Actually, I was more afraid that he'd try to compete with me. As I went up and down, I imagined the half-pipe was full of my species, their tentacles bobbling with every pass they were making.

I decided I shouldn't hold back, even though my conscience told me I was being really selfish. I argued back that it wouldn't be fair to me if I didn't do all I was capable of. Besides, Willy was my friend. He should be happy for me. I wanted to try an alley-oop, or maybe, if I dared, even a rodeo-flip. I let myself bonk on top and then tried each one of the tricks I'd seen the other boarders do that afternoon.

I now knew what I was going to do with my life. I'd follow the snowboarding competitions all over the world until I was at least a hundred and thirteen. And then I'd be a coach.

All of a sudden, I realized how quiet it was, and *then* I realized that I was the only one on the pipe. I slowed, rocking back and forth lower and lower on the sides. Everyone was watching me, and when I came to a stop, they broke into cheers.

I loved being the center of attention. Maybe this was the feeling Alicia craved. The sun seemed to gleam a little brighter on the snow, but then I saw how miserable Willy looked.

I got off and went over to him.

"What would you like to do now?" I asked, a bit awkwardly.

"Nothing," he snapped. He turned his back on me and boarded the rest of the way down the slope.

I followed Willy all the way down the slope, careful not to overtake him, and then into the lodge. I took a second to check my tentacle status. They seemed to want to stay inside my head, so I yanked off my helmet and then my parka and looked around for Willy. Instead, I saw my dad leaning against a post with his arms crossed, looking like he wanted to murder me.

"What were you thinking, Deborah?" he asked. "How many times have I told you not to draw attention to yourself?"

"You were watching?"

"You're darn right I was watching, from the balcony with fifty other people."

"I was just having fun. Why can't you be proud of me?"

We heard someone clear her throat behind us.

"Excuse me?" she said. We both turned. She was the snowboarding girl I'd admired earlier. She had long, dark hair, and her lips were chapped. "I just wanted to say that your daughter has real talent."

I was afraid Dad was going to be rude, but he softened a bit.

"Thank you."

"You haven't been here before, have you?" She smiled at me. "Where did you learn to do that? I never saw anyone fakie like you."

"Do what?" I asked.

"You know, ride backward," she answered. "I mean, you caught air like no one I've ever seen."

"I . . ."

Dad found his grumpy old self again and grabbed my arm.

"We were just leaving," he said, dragging me away.

"Oh," the girl said, taken aback for a second by Dad's tone of voice. But then she called out to me, "You really rock."

Dad was being absolutely ridiculous. I would have thought up a good story to tell the girl, like we were from Lithuania.

"Thanks," I called back over my shoulder. "You do, too."

She gave me a thumbs-up, put on some lip balm, and walked away in the opposite direction.

"Hey, George, Deborah."

Fred waved at us. He and Margie walked over with Willy, whose glum face mirrored mine.

"Deborah, we saw you on the pipe. You're awesome," Margie said. "We were just going to have a snack. I know you have dietary restrictions, but you're welcome to join us."

Willy wouldn't look at me.

"Oh, come on, Dad," I pleaded. Maybe I could get Willy talking to me again.

Dad had calmed down by now. He really is a softy. "Oh, all right," he said, and then added for the Logans' sake, "but no more tricks like those. I don't want you to get hurt."

We went into the restaurant. Fred ordered hamburgers and milk shakes for the whole family. Dad and I popped our green tablets in our mouths, and then I stared at the glass of water in front of me. Fred and Dad started talking about golf, of all things. Margie made small talk with me, but she could tell that I wasn't in the mood, so she stopped trying.

Willy and I sat there and brooded. I was getting angrier by the moment. He was such a baby. He might as well face the fact that I was superior to him. In a few weeks my species would be in charge, and he'd have to wake up and smell the cocoa anyway.

I hoped that all the ships would crash in the meteor belt on their way here. (I didn't care if I was contradicting myself.) I was sick and tired of living my life for the Home World. I was an American girl, even if I had three stomachs.

Willy ripped into his hamburger. I contemplated the little bits of meat that fell to his plate. What was so delicious about dead cows anyway? What did cocoa taste like? Would a green salad *really* kill me?

We didn't stay long in the restaurant. That afternoon Fred got Dad on the slopes. Margie said she had enough skiing and was going to read by the fireplace. I had no idea where Willy went.

I wandered into the store, and, as though I were in a trance, I found myself standing in front of the candy counter. My hand reached out, and I made a decision that would change me forever.

Chapter Nine

Forbidden Delights

My fingers traced a yellow package of peanut M&Ms. I almost chose them, but then I remembered reading a surprising number of people are allergic to peanuts. I wasn't human, but picking a food with a proven death trail didn't seem like a good idea.

I fingered a Mars Bar, and then a Peppermint Pattie, but the M&Ms kept calling my name. Should I get the almond kind? Or the dark chocolate ones?

I felt like a doofus standing there, so I grabbed a bag of regular M&Ms. Might as well start with the simplest poison, I thought.

At the cash register, a teenage boy in an absurdly huge parka was ahead of me. He took forever to pay, searching for change through what seemed like twenty pockets. I almost chickened out and had just turned around to return the candy when the boy finally said, "Dude, I found it."

He paid for his orange juice and was out of there. I stepped up to the counter shaking so much I dropped two quarters on the floor. As I squatted down to pick up the change, I realized I was sweating. Had the ski lodge suddenly turned up the heat? Or was the candy already oozing something toxic to my system through the wrapper?

I stood up and pushed my money across the counter to the cashier as fast as I could. The cash register drawer sprang open, and I knew I was committed.

I went back into the lobby in a kind of a daze, nervously rolling the M&Ms around inside the bag. I wondered what would happen if I tore open the wrapper then and there and stuffed all of them inside my mouth. Would I projectile vomit? Writhe, gasping for air, on the floor?

Or would I die with less drama? I imagined turning pale and being carried over to the sofa where Margie was reading her novel, gently expiring in front of the blazing fire, my hand dropping toward the floor, unleashing the last red M&M from my grasp. I saw it roll to a dead stop in front of my father's feet as he rushed to my side, his shoes leaving wet footprints on the hardwood floor.

I sighed and tucked the candy inside my pocket. All I wanted was to be normal, to enjoy food instead of having to binge every October thirty-first, to eat something other than a human at least once in my life.

So what if Willy's family was into horror. Today they were just an average American family spending lots of money and having a good time, leaving their coffins at home and their vampire capes stored away.

I wanted to forget about the great invasion and feast. I wasn't hungry now, but I really, really didn't want to eat people at all anymore.

I sat down next to Margie. She looked up from her book.

"You and Willy had a fight?" she asked.

"I guess," I said. "He started to act weird all of a sudden."

"You know, Deborah, Willy can be pretty competitive. I think he wanted to show off for you, but when he saw what a natural you are at snowboarding, his ego couldn't handle it. Give it a little time. Things will work out between the two of you."

Snowboarding felt like breathing to me, like flying. Why didn't Willy understand?

"I'm not going to pretend I'm not good at something when I am," I told Margie.

"Good for you," Margie said. "You need to be true to yourself, Deborah."

I saw Willy walking toward us, his hands deep in his jacket pockets. I could tell he was still mad by the way he was wrinkling his forehead. He was lost in his own world and didn't see me sitting with Margie until he was almost stepping on my toes.

You'd have thought I'd just morphed into Alicia by the look he gave me.

Margie noticed his mood, too, and sighed.

"I ran out of quarters," he said. "Can I have more for the arcade?"

"I'm out of change, so you're going to have to sit here until Fred gets off the slopes," Margie said. "Do you want to talk things over with Deborah?"

He gave me a sideways glance. "No."

"Are you sure?" she asked, giving him another chance.

"No," Willy repeated.

"Have it your way," Margie said, and opened her book again.

Willy slunk down in the chair next to me, crossing his arms, and stared at the floor. I crossed my arms, too, closed my eyes, and tried to ignore him as best I could, the M&Ms like venom in my pocket.

An hour later Dad and I were heading back to Prattville. I fell asleep before we'd gone twenty miles. I dreamed of spaceships descending on my school, blasting the roof off my classroom with laserlike rays, and my species descending down metal ramps with tentacles fully extended and knives and forks at the ready. A tentacle curled around Willy's waist. To my horror, I saw that it belonged to me.

I woke with a start. Dad was whistling. I sat up, rubbed my eyes, and saw we were almost home.

"You must have worn yourself out, young lady," he said. "You've been sleeping for a couple of hours."

He was in a good mood. I could see a slight suntan line where his ski goggles had been.

"Did you have fun?" I asked.

"I believe I did," he said, considering my question. "Who would have imagined?"

"Are you still mad at me?"

"No, darling." He patted my hand. "I could never stay mad at you. You just have to be patient a little bit longer. Next winter you can snowboard to your heart's content." He chuckled. "I imagine there will be competitions in no time. All the young people will want to do it, and you, my little *nmchklt*, will lead the way."

My mood instantly turned sour. He hadn't called me a *nmchklt* since I was seven. What was this all about? What happened to "You're almost a woman now, and oh, by the way, you're marrying pimple-faced Gerald?" I was too tired to protest; brooding was much easier. I fluffed up my parka and used it as a pillow, pretending to sleep the rest of the way.

As we rolled into the driveway, I could see the living room glowing with candlelight. I lugged my stuff into the house to find Jimmy Joe Crawford's voice twanging softly from the speakers, and Mom dozing on the couch with a funny smile on her face.

"Home from the slopes, dear," Dad announced as he followed me inside. He chuckled. "I hate to tear you away from Jimmy Joe."

Mom jolted up.

"Oh," she said, straightening her hair. "I didn't expect you back so soon."

I was fully awake now and feeling indignant all over again. How dare Dad call me a *nmchklt*. Especially after all of the talk about how I was growing up: duty and career and betrothal and blah, blah, blah.

I shuddered. Gerald was nice, but he was a nerd. I wanted to go on a date with a human boy. Up until a few hours ago, I wanted that boy to be Willy.

"The ski lodge police got me," I told Mom. "Dad didn't like how I was snowboarding, and Willy probably will never talk to me again."

I hadn't intended to imply that my problems

with Willy were Dad's fault, but I let my mom think the worst.

"You said you were going to let her have fun," Mom said. The candlelight seemed to flicker a little faster, as Jimmy Joe belted out "My Baby Knocked Me Out in the Boxing Ring of Love."

"You should have seen what she was doing, Virginia," Dad said. "She might as well have been on ESPN with all the attention she was drawing to herself."

Dad's ski hat was elevating, so I ducked out and went to my room. I started my computer to IM Willy. He wasn't online, and I had to resort to e-mail.

I clicked on CREATE MAIL and almost apologized, but then I thought, *Apologize for what?* I wrote this instead:

> Willy,
> The way you acted today was ridiculous.
> Deborah

I sent it off and then flopped down on my bed and stared at the ceiling. Willy was the one who needed to grow up. Somebody was always going to be better than he was at something. Willy was talented on the sax. Why couldn't he be happy with that?

My parents' voices were getting louder. I heard Dad say, "For the last time, I have no idea what happened between her and Willy."

"Will the two of you be quiet?" The front door slammed. Grandmother was back. "I have to do some important calculations immediately. And turn off that vaporous racket." Evidently she wasn't a country music fan.

I stood at my door and listened.

"The atmosphere of this planet is so thin I need to rework the reentry angles of our ships. There's not enough friction to slow the larger ships down. Something the two of you failed to report, I might add," Grandmother scolded my parents.

Stan spoke then. "But we also have good news. We've found the perfect place for the—"

Grandmother and my parents said "Shhh" at the same time, like a chorus. Mom's voice got very quiet. I strained to listen, but I was sure she said, "Deborah might hear."

Whatever they were talking about, it sounded like I was going to spend my winter break in southern Nevada in a place that looked like the surface of the moon.

A minute later I was lugging my pillow, my pajamas, and a quilt from my bed into the living room.

My parents headed to their room, still arguing, but in whispers now. Stan and Gerald were in the den fighting about how to set up the hide-a-bed. I sat on the couch next to where I'd thrown my jacket. I started to toss it on a chair, but I heard the crackle of the M&Ms in my pocket.

I took out the package and brought it to my nose. I could almost smell chocolate through the wrapper. I slipped the bag back into the pocket until the house quieted.

Around midnight, I got the M&Ms out and ripped off the back corner of the package. Every chamber of my heart was beating overtime. It felt dangerous, like smoking, but not so disgusting.

I poured out three M&Ms onto my hand. They looked so innocent. Would they really kill me? I couldn't think of any scientific studies my parents ever mentioned that would support the theory. My hand trembled as I lifted them to my mouth. I stuck my tongue out and licked the green one.

The taste was so strange. Bitter? Sweet? I had no idea. I sweated like I did when I bought the candy, but other than that, my body seemed fine. I bit down on the M&M and held it on my tongue.

I couldn't feel any poison flowing into my bloodstream. I debated whether to spit it out, but the sweetness and chocolate spread across my tongue, and I didn't want to waste the experience in case I never tried another.

It took over a minute before I got up the nerve to swallow. By then the candy was almost dissolved. Down the hatch it went.

I waited to see if I was going to have an allergic reaction. My breathing was okay. I went into the bathroom off the kitchen to see if there were any splotches on my face. The same old me stared back from the mirror. I was fine.

In fact, I was more than fine. Chocolate was almost as good as the taste of essence. Around one o'clock, I let myself have another M&M, and then another. My parents were criminals for making me miss this wonderful taste all my life.

A few minutes later I'd gobbled up the rest of the bag.

I shoved the wrapper as far as I could into the inside

pocket of my jacket, to throw away later. I tried to sleep, but I couldn't, thinking of the two new sensations I'd had that day, the thrill of catching air over the snow, and the taste of chocolate on my tongue. What other sports should I try? Water-skiing? Bungee jumping?

And what else could I eat? My pillow was wet from saliva.

On Sunday, I checked my IM every hour. I hoped that Willy would at least send me an angry message back, but he either wasn't online or had decided to hide it if he was.

My inbox also stayed empty. I told myself that maybe the Logans had spent the night at Sky Ridge, but when I checked one last time before bed there was still nothing.

At school Alicia and Amanda were sitting on the desks that surrounded Willy's. He was enjoying the attention. Amanda now had braces; she'd whined enough about her overbite that her parents had given in. I pitied her. I had good teeth (*all* of them), and I didn't need to be Alicia's friend.

Alicia was holding a newspaper and had evidently just finished reading an article from the *Prattville Gazette*. Mr. Bartlett had been writing the day's agenda on the whiteboard, and whatever it was she read had upset him.

"I don't need a celebrity in my classroom," he said. His handwriting had gotten really huge, and he had to erase everything and start over from the beginning.

I put my backpack next to my chair and pretended

I wasn't interested. I had to sharpen my pencils, though, and the sharpener just happened to be near Alicia. I saw the newspaper headline on her desk.

Vampire Boy's Trial Today

I'd been so absorbed with snowboarding that I had hardly listened when Willy mentioned the trial on the lift. He was going to be known from now on as Vampire Boy wherever he went. I couldn't imagine the disgrace of having your family's peculiarities broadcast for the entire town to laugh at. Back home, they'd have to sacrifice themselves.

Right now, though, he was eating up all the attention.

"Yeah, my parents are signing me out of school today at ten-thirty," Willy said. "You don't think I'm ridiculous, do you, Alicia?"

"I think you're so cool," Alicia said. "My parents don't even want me to talk to you."

She smiled as though disobeying them gave her a great amount of pleasure. Willy's remark felt like a low blow to me. My eyes smarted, but I was one tough human-eating machine. I would not cry. No sissy red tears would fall.

Over the next few days, I decided to ignore Willy as much as I could. This was harder to do with Alicia as we had to work together.

"Chen, would you tell Alicia that the square root of 1296 isn't 34, it's 36."

"Chen, would you tell Alicia that I'm transmitting her address to the first wave of ships that will be landing."

Okay, that second thing was just a fantasy, but I thought Mom might be willing to send the message if I asked politely.

Chen got tired of being the messenger after the first couple of times. When I continued to ignore Alicia, she tattled to Mr. Bartlett and I got another detention.

Every so often, I caught Willy glancing at me. Of course, he caught me looking at him. Each time our eyes met, we quickly turned away..

Chapter Ten

Bathroom Issues

Istarted my exploration of the Earth diet in earnest. On Monday after serving my new detention, I bought a Snickers bar at the Quick-Mart. I thought I owed myself chocolate after spending an extra hour with Mr. Bartlett.

The Snickers was kind of disgusting at first, chewy in the middle with the little pieces of peanuts, but I told myself to think of it as brains and then it went right down. For the next three afternoons I concentrated on ice cream. From the first taste, I couldn't believe it had been denied to me for almost twelve years. I *loved* ice cream, especially strawberry. I tried potato chips on Friday and found them divine. They were salty the way blood is but so much more convenient to get.

Then I began to stop at the supermarket. I tried mangos, oranges, low-fat yogurt for a protein source.

My problem was that I always felt guilty after eating. Every time. That was the weird thing. I felt I was lying, though I wasn't sure to whom. My parents? I couldn't see how what I was doing could be wrong, but I knew how disappointed they would be in me if they found out.

I kept asking myself questions about the future. If my parents knew that eating human food was as safe as eating humans, would they help to change Home World policies? I understood we were a species who conquered worlds. Conquering inferior species was what we did, but was it too bizarre to think that we might be compassionate conquerors?

I finally admitted I indulged for another reason: to keep my mind off Willy. He was doing the unthinkable, eating lunch with Alicia.

Later that week, our credit-card bill came, and Dad's tentacles shot up so fast, his hat hit the ceiling. I guess our trip to Sky Ridge was a drop in the bucket compared to the Hummer and Mom's gambling at the Lucky Nugget.

Mom tried to soothe his nerves. "Just send in the minimum payment, George. By this time next month, the bill won't matter."

"The invasion better not fail or we'll go bankrupt," Dad grumbled.

Mom drove me bonkers listening to Jimmy Joe Crawford both day and night. That alone might make a girl eat. Grandmother's eyes got really small, like she got a headache, every time Mom put on the CD. Dad's tolerance of Mom's crush on Jimmy Joe had been pretty high, but by the 754th time she played the *Blue Jeans and Roses* CD, he started muttering and went out to the garage to fiddle with the Impala.

For reasons beyond me, Gerald and Stan became Jimmy Joe fans. Gerald even got a black cowboy hat, just like Jimmy Joe's. I thought he looked like a dork. I wanted to tell him this was California, not Texas, but I was raised to be polite, so I kept my mouth shut.

One afternoon I came home to find Mom and the boys singing along to "Love Me, Love My Truck," packing my mom's Avon orders in bags covered in candy canes and snowflakes. They seemed particularly excited.

"What's up?" I asked.

"Oh, darling." Mom jumped up and kissed me, her tentacles extending to embrace me. I wiped my cheek and Plum Shadow Shine Supreme lipstick came off on my hand. "You know that Jimmy Joe is not going to put on any more concerts after this year."

"Yeah?" I asked suspiciously.

"Your grandmother saw how upset I was, and, you'll never guess . . . She's taking Stan, Gerald, and me to see Jimmy Joe's big blowout concert at Sho-Sho-Pah Casino for New Year's Eve."

"This was Grandmother's idea? Does Dad know?"

"I thought I'd tell him at the last minute. You know, so he won't worry."

"About your little problem?" I asked as diplomatically as I could.

"All of that is behind me. We're only going for dinner and the show. I won't touch even a slot machine, I promise."

Jimmy Joe + New Year's Eve ≒ Grandmother. What was she up to?

On the Tuesday before vacation started, Mr. Bartlett was called to be a witness at Willy's trial. We had a sub, the first one all year, because Mr. Bartlett never missed a day of school. He was especially vain about his robust health. At least once a week, he'd announce, "If you ate raw food, I wouldn't have to deal with all these absence notes from your parents."

Willy wasn't at school either. Alicia said that after Mr. Bartlett's testimony, the attorneys would give their closing arguments. Fred and Margie wanted him to hear those. Was she so chummy with Willy that he told her all the details of the case? During silent reading, I snapped a pencil in two, thinking about them talking on the phone, sending e-mails, holding hands . . .

Then, out of nowhere, I got the strangest sensation.

There's something I've avoided talking about because I haven't been able to figure out how to mention it politely. Let me put it this way: what goes in must come out. Because my species takes a long time digesting our food, we really don't need to use the bathroom until nine months or so after we've fed. Our bodies absorb all fluids, so we don't ever have to use the toilet for the other reason.

Actually, our alimentary canals aren't that much different from humans', other than the fact we have three stomachs (like a cow, I know.) To make a long story short, we use the bathroom almost the same way as humans do, except just once a year, and boy, do we use it. That's why I was so surprised when I needed to go. I hadn't figured my new diet would pass through me so fast.

And then I needed to go again during science, and then right before band practice, and then again as we walked out to P.E.

Ms. Martinez was waiting for me outside the bathroom door. "Are you okay?" she asked.

"Um, I just need . . ."

I couldn't think what humans took for this sort of thing.

"Pepto-Bismol?" she asked.

By the time I got home, I was okay, or so I thought, but as soon as I woke up the next morning I needed to go again. I put on the shower full blast and hoped no one heard the toilet flush.

Mom and Dad were reading the newspaper when I came out of the bathroom.

"Was that the toilet I heard?" Dad asked.

My mind went blank. What was I going to say? Should I tell them then and there what I'd been doing?

"Deborah, you can take off your hat," Mom said.

"Huh?" I asked.

"Your Tentacle Disruption Syndrome won't bother you anymore," she said. "You're in phase two now, Frequent Elimination Pattern."

I was relieved to know that my body was reacting to hormones and not my new diet, but I still didn't want my bathroom habits spoken of like they were a puberty progress report. Dad went back to his paper, evidently as embarrassed as I was.

"I'm going to school," I said.

Both Willy and Mr. Bartlett were gone again. Most classes are awful when their teacher is away, but we were so grateful to have a nice one for a change that we did everything to be good for Ms. Martinez. Except for Alicia, that is. She got her name on the board twice for being rude. Boy, was Alicia surprised when Ms. Martinez handed her an essay about respect that she had to copy over during P.E.

Luckily I only had to take one trip to the bathroom and that was during lunch recess. I knew the true test for my dietary experiments was going to be meat. Hamburger, chicken, pork, salmon—the possibilities were endless. If I found out meat was safe, then I might take the chance of coming clean with my parents. Surely then they'd help me save humanity.

After school I decided the time had come. I rode my bike to Monterey Avenue, where the strip malls and burger joints were. When I got to Burger King, I locked my bike in the rack and stood there for a good minute before I went inside.

I wasn't as afraid as I was with the M&Ms, but I was still nervous. If I could eat meat, I could eat anything. Or it might be the one food that would finally do me in.

The girl at the counter chewed gum as I placed my order, one plain Whopper. I wanted the pure experience. Ketchup and pickles could wait until later.

After I got the burger, I sat down at a small table and took a whiff. Charbroiled dead cow flooded my senses. The aroma was so potent I felt dizzy. Meat was life, and my body was in complete response.

I took a small bite and held the bread and meat in my mouth like I had with the green M&M. I was in ecstasy. The cow had been terrified as it was slaughtered, and its essence was strong and full of flavor. I could barely contain myself. I chewed slowly, savoring every sensation.

Before I could take a second bite, Alicia walked in with her family. She wore a mauve leotard and pink tights. Her brown hair was in a tight bun surrounded with a tiara full of rhinestones.

One part of me watched her as another kept watch on

my vital signs. She turned around and saw me.

"Hi, Deborah."

Alicia waved and smiled like she was about to invite me to a slumber party. She almost skipped over and sat down on the chair across from mine, her braces shining.

"What about your allergies?" she asked.

"I . . . I . . ."

"Allergy shots?"

"Yeah," I said.

She pointed to her crown. "I've been the Prattville Gymnastic Queen for the last two years," she said, her voice just a little too loud. The old woman sipping her coffee in the booth next to us stared. "We're on the way to the biggest competition of the year. Mom says I'll keep the crown this year, too."

I squeezed the hamburger bun so hard my fingers were making indentations.

"Congratulations," I said. Alicia kept smiling at me, and I realized she was expecting me to say something else. "Nice rhinestones."

"They're *real*," she said. "Do you think the Math Champ Crown will have some when I win it?"

If Alicia had belonged to my species, she easily could have been the next Most Supreme Imperial High Matriarch. Her personality fit the job description to a T.

"Alicia, our shakes are ready," her father said. "Time to go."

There he was, evil school board man, part of the school administration that gave Willy such a hard time expressing who he was.

Alicia stood up. "By the way, I just found out Willy lost

106

the case. I thought he might be famous, but he really is a loser."

I wanted to take my Whopper and shove it in her face. I wanted to devour her, her dad, and the whole restaurant. I needed all of my strength to keep my tentacles from popping straight out of my head.

"Willy is my friend," I said.

"Your loss."

With that she flounced back to her parents. She whispered something to them and they both glanced at me.

My hamburger tasted delicious, but I hardly cared.

The next morning Dad woke me up whistling.

I sat up on the couch and rubbed my eyes. "You sound awfully happy," I said.

"We have a date." Mom walked into the living room, and Dad took her in his arms, spun her around, and starting to sing, "We have a date, we have a date, we have a date for the invasion."

"Oh, my gosh," I said, jumping up. "When?"

"January seventeenth," Dad said, dipping Mom back like they do in the movies.

"Will the three of you quiet down?" Grandmother called from my room. "You might as well announce the invasion to the whole neighborhood."

"But that's the day of the math contest," I said.

"Don't worry," Mom said. "The invasion won't happen until late in the evening. You'll have plenty of time to defeat the other sixth graders."

"And have the crown to show off when Her Most Supreme Imperial High Matriarch arrives," Dad said proudly.

Stan and Gerald came out of the den and, when they heard the news, they shouted, "Home World, Home World, Home World," the way fans say USA, USA, USA at international athletic events.

Grandmother threw a shoe from my bedroom doorway and hit Stan on the head. We all started to giggle, except for Stan. Grandmother has a mean arm.

I left for school in a better mood than I'd been in since my encounter with Alicia. It was the last day before vacation, and I was determined to make up everything with Willy. Now that Alicia had turned traitor on him, he was going to need a real friend.

I found him leaning against the wall next to the water fountains, near the cafeteria looking forlorn.

"Look," I said. He turned his head away. "I'm sorry for what I said, and I'm sorry you lost the case."

He was silent for a moment, and I wondered if he'd let me make up with him.

"Margie and Dad say I take things too personally," he finally said, still staring at the puddle stain beneath the water fountain.

"You know, Willy, you are the best musician in the band."

He turned his head my way. "Deborah, don't suck up."

"I'm not. I'm telling you the truth."

Mr. Spencer had finally seen the light about Willy. He asked him to play a riff on his sax, something improvised on the spot. He used the basic melody of "My Favorite Things," but every time he played he morphed the tune in a different way.

"Yeah, well, I wish it was true," Willy said. "Margie and Dad are putting on this horror movie festival at the

Crest Theater in Sacramento. They're working with the ACLU to raise money for causes like mine. People are going to come in costumes and everything. The only bad part is that they want me to play my sax for this old silent movie clip."

"That's great," I said.

"Stuff it, Deborah."

I ignored his comment. "When's it going to happen?"

"January seventeenth, the same day as Math Champs. It was the only day that my dad could book the theater," he said.

"If you can't come to Math Champs, it's okay." I realized that I really did want him there. Math Champs would be the last normal moment we'd have. Willy must have heard the disappointment in my voice.

"Liar," he said, smiling at last. "The festival doesn't start until eight, so maybe I can come."

"Okay," I said.

My heart broke as I smiled back. If there was just some way I could tell him what the real horror festival was going to be, I'd have said, "Run for your life." Unfortunately, there'd be no place for Willy to hide.

That evening was our school's annual "Celebration of Culture," which took the place of what used to be the Christmas program. A few of the highlights were a fourth-grade play about the seven principles of Kwanzaa, the entire second grade performing a traditional Hmong dance, and kindergartners pretending they were whirling dervishes. Ms. Henderson even had her first graders recite a poem about the solstice.

The band played "Silent Night," "The Dreidl Song,"

and then we finished with "My Favorite Things." The audience cheered when Willy began. His eyes were closed like he was feeling the music. When his last notes trailed away, the audience went wild.

I had just enough time to whisper to Willy, "Now do you believe me?"

He didn't say anything but just gave me his wonderful smile.

Chapter Eleven

Supper at Sho-Sho-Pah

I had mixed feelings about my parents being on the Supreme High Council. On one hand, it would mean that I'd get a lot of attention, which I'd hate. I'd be expected to be a role model. Gerald and I would be followed by Home World paparazzi, and there would be pictures of us feeding on hapless Earthlings in all the magazines. If I refused to feed, I'd put my parents' chances for advancement in jeopardy, if they weren't executed for raising such an obstinate daughter.

On the other hand, Mom and Dad would have a lot of power if they became members. There would be more of a chance of changing policies if I convinced them our diet could be modified.

Grandmother had confirmed there were big plans for Earth. A new policy would be put into place once the invasion was accomplished. Instead of feeding on the entire population like a herd of locusts, we were now going to try to keep a sizable number of people alive to replenish the food supply. I guess we learned a lesson after gobbling up the frog planet so quickly.

It takes a considerable amount of time for humans to grow big enough to make a decent-size meal, but until we found another planet inhabited with faster-growing species, human beings were going to have to last.

Mom and Dad were sure that a new seat on the council would have to be made to oversee the management of all this. And who else knew more about Earth and its people? If one of my parents were selected, when it was time to retire, I'd inherit the position and all the privileges that went with it.

I doubted my species would ever give up their love of essence, the taste of the frog people, or humans of Earth, or any other sentient species they could lay their hands on. But I had to keep dreaming. I remembered the terror of the cow in the hamburger I'd eaten.

I decided I needed to try as many types of meat as possible. The more data I had, the better. Maybe I'd tell Stan and Gerald first. If they were going to run a franchise, did it have to serve humans exclusively? Perhaps they could get the Home Worlders warmed up to the idea of chicken nuggets. Maybe offer a two-for-one deal.

Powerful women like Grandmother would be the hardest to convince, because they had the most to lose. If something as elemental as hunting and feeding was challenged, who could say what else might change?

There was one thing Grandmother had no control over, and that was me. I'd grown half an inch since school had started. My overskin actually ached a bit because it was being stretched so quickly.

At least the bathroom issue was improving. The Whopper seemed to be the charm. My digestion slowed down after I tried it. Mom said I'd passed through phase two really fast.

So I decided to continue my experiments with the Earth diet. Every afternoon I grabbed a few bucks from my piggy bank and went out on my bike.

A little-known fact: pork tastes just like human. I did comparison checks of Big Macs and Wendy's Bacon Cheeseburger, but the pork loin sandwich I had at Figueroa's deli beat them all. The pig was so intelligent that I doubt the folks from home could tell the difference between it and the average Joe on the street.

The day I discovered the delights of the pork loin sandwich, I officially found out we would be spending most of my winter break in Desolation, Nevada, to do the set-up work for the invasion.

There were several "hot spots," as Dad called them, around the world. New York, Moscow, London, Hong Kong, and Santiago, Chile, had the right conditions for communications. Ships were going to land in these places first, but the abandoned Oasis Motel on Route 375 in Nevada and our house in Prattville were in just the right locations to create an arc of gamma rays that would disrupt all of Earth's communication.

When we returned to Prattville, Gerald would stay at the Oasis and he and Mom would bounce the rays back and forth to amplify their intensity.

I know it was a stressful time for my parents. They'd lived far away from home for eleven years, working to support me and pay the mortgage while doing all the groundwork necessary for the invasion, and now the big moment was just around the corner.

But something else was going on. Both Mom and

Dad kept giving me these dopey looks and then they'd look really sad. More than once I'd hear my name, then a whole bunch of whispering that I could never make out. When I'd walk into the room, everyone would stop talking.

I found Gerald in our backyard on Christmas Eve working at our picnic table on a small model of a laser.

"I know something's up," I said. "As my fiancé, I think you're obligated to tell me. We're going to the Oasis for more than just invasion preparation, and it has to do with me, doesn't it?"

Just as I asked this, Grandmother walked out of the shed where Dad kept the lawn mower and a spare intergalactic relay monitor. "Stop asking questions," she said. "That's an order."

Gerald adjusted a mirror on his model until I could see his face reflecting in its surface. His look told me that I'd better do as I was told.

On the morning of New Year's Eve, I found Grandmother in the kitchen making some sort of gloppy purple stuff on the stove that smelled like the dirty-clothes hamper.

"What's that for?" I asked.

"Ancient beauty secret," she said.

"You're kidding me."

"I never kid. Your mother has this silly Avon business. I want to remind her of the old ways."

I was about to tell her that Mom was a very good businesswoman and she had fun selling the products. What was so wrong with that? Just then I got a whiff of what was in the pot, and the banana I'd eaten for breakfast almost came up. I felt the same way I did when all six of my tentacles vomited after we fed on some heroin addicts when I was three.

"This stuff really stinks."

"You've been too conditioned by Earth odors," Grandmother retorted. She stuck a spoon into the boiling mess. It stood straight up. "Ah, it's ready."

"Grandmother, you can't stand Jimmy Joe Crawford, so why are you taking Mom to his concert?"

She stopped pouring the glop. The way she looked at me made me feel like I'd just asked her to give the attack plan for Invasion Day to the United Nations.

"You ask a lot of questions for a *nmchklt*."

Mom was fluttery all day. Around three o'clock, she and Grandmother both had the purple glop on their faces.

"You could wear that for next Halloween," Dad told them. "It beats our tentacles for scaring people."

He wasn't thrilled about their going to the concert. They ignored him. I said good-bye, careful to stay out of their way in case Grandmother got the idea of putting some on my face.

Right before they left, Dad lectured Mom about the vice of gambling.

"I've told you a hundred times, George, I'm over it," she said.

Gerald had a black cowboy hat of his own by now. Stan offered an arm to Mom as they walked out the door. Gerald tried to escort Grandmother, but she hit him with her purse.

After they left, Dad and I watched the New Year celebrations on TV. I tried to stay awake to find out about the concert, but they hadn't returned by the time the ball dropped in Times Square and Dad told me to hit the sack.

The next morning I found Mom at the kitchen table, her head in her hands, sobbing over the front page of the *Prattville Gazette*. *Uh-oh,* I thought. *She's done it again, and we'll have to sell the house to pay her gambling debts.*

I tugged the front page from beneath her elbows and read the bad news:

JIMMY JOE CRAWFORD VICTIM OF CANNIBAL MURDERER

My stomachs flip-flopped as I scanned the article. Jimmy Joe's manager had found his little finger and an ankle next to his guitar in his dressing room. He also found his ruby pinky ring that led to the identification, along with various items that belonged to his two body-guards.

"There is a likely relationship between Mr. Crawford's and his bodyguards' deaths, the rest stop murders, and the murders at the Lucky Nugget Casino, as Mr. Crawford was playing at the casino the night— weeks ago—that two people there were killed," Agent Mackenzie was reported to say. "The types of bite marks were the same in all three cases; however, they do not fit any known human or animal's."

She refused to speculate why the bite marks were so strange.

"You ate Jimmy Joe?" I asked Mom.

This made her bawl even harder. It was a stupid question because I knew who still hadn't fed.

"Where's Grandmother?" I asked.

"I'll . . . never . . . trust . . . her . . . again," Mom said between sobs. She reached for a tissue, and I jumped back.

"Mom, what happened to your face?"

"It's all Mother's fault," Mom said, wiping her eyes. Red tears were streaking down her green leathery face like icing melting on a Christmas cookie. "She insisted I use her beauty secret, and it did this to me. The cream sloughed off my human overskin."

I grew up with the picture in my bedroom of the three of us before we were modified, but I'd never come face-to-face with our species' looks in person. I've always thought that our tentacles were kind of cool, but I had no idea what they were attached to was *this* disgusting.

I took a deep breath, then sat down and patted her hand. "What happened last night?"

"She said we had backstage passes. I didn't realize that the beauty cream was calculated to work just as the concert was over. I'll never forget the look on Jimmy Joe's face when his bodyguard opened the door." Mom was slowly calming down. "Mother said extra terror before an invasion is always a good thing."

"Where were Stan and Gerald during all of this?"

"Playing keno. They didn't know what happened until they met us at our car." She sighed. "Your father got up early and doesn't know anything about this. He's going to be furious."

The doorbell rang. I wondered how they got out of the casino with no one noticing. There had to have been surveillance cameras all over the place.

"I'll get it," I said, and handed Mom another tissue.

I looked out the window before I opened the door.

Margie and Willy were standing there. Margie had her hand on his shoulder and he was holding a present.

"Uh, hi," I said, as I slid out the door, closing it behind me.

"Happy New Year, Deborah," Margie said. "We came by because . . . the last month has been difficult with the trial. . . ." Margie's eyes welled up. "We just wanted you to know how important your friendship with Willy is to all of us."

Oh, please, I thought, *not two crying moms.*

Willy looked self-conscious. He kpet his eyes on the ground, and I could feel his embarrassment.

"I overheard Alicia tell Amanda you're not allergic anymore, so I got you . . . I mean, we got you a treat."

He handed me a small red box with a gold ribbon.

"Thank you," I said.

Mom told her Avon customers good things come in small packages.

"I am so glad the two of you made up," Margie said, sounding relieved. "Deborah, could I talk to Virginia?"

"To Mom?" I asked a little too loudly. "Well, she's sick."

"Oh, darn. I really want to get together with her. Tell her I'll call, will you?"

I was trying to think of a way to say good-bye and get back into the house, but then Willy's face lit up.

"Have you seen the news this morning?"

"Just the paper."

"Well, you know, that country singer Jimmy Joe what's it?"

"Crawford," I said as calmly as I could. "He died, didn't he?"

"They have this really neat video of the people they think killed him. They have these masks on, only they might not be people at all but monsters or aliens. And we heard on the radio that somebody at the police lab leaked the fact that they found DNA at all three places the people have been killed at, and, get this, it doesn't match anything on Earth."

"Fascinating," I said, feeling for the doorknob.

"The reporter said they could be from outer space," Margie said, and then she shivered. "I prefer my bloodthirsty aliens on a movie screen. Anyway, Deborah, tell Virginia that I hope she gets better soon."

"Okay," I said.

"I'll wait in the car," Margie told Willy.

Willy waited until she was out of earshot before he said anything. "Margie and Dad said that I have to say I'm sorry for getting mad at you. I just wanted to be good at something, and then when I saw that you were such a natural at snowboarding I hated you for a little while."

"Willy, you're great the way you are," I said.

He shook his head. "You're good at school, and you're good at sports. I suck at both. But I've missed being your friend, so I guess I'll just have to put up with how perfect you are."

He smiled a little, like we were sharing a secret.

"Can I open my present now?" I asked.

"Yeah," he said.

I peeled off the wrapping. A giant chocolate kiss covered by gold foil was snuggled inside.

"I love it," I said.

I really did.

"I thought you might," he said, and then ran to the waiting car.

Willy was smarter than I thought.

Discretely hiding my kiss in my sweatshirt pocket, I walked back inside. Dad was flipping from one channel to the next. All the local stations were showing the same video from the casino. He turned to CNN and stopped. Evidently the networks were picking up the story.

The time on the video read 1:13 A.M., well after the concert. In grainy footage, there appeared what looked like the backs of two women who were walking down a hallway. A big, hulking man dressed in an exquisite suit stood in front of a door, and then a look of terror crossed his face.

The lankier woman pushed him backward, causing the door to cave in. The other woman crumpled in the hallway and hid her head in her arms.

For the next four minutes the camera taped the gaping door and the woman on the floor. She raised her head once and looked, then just as quickly hid her eyes again. A few minutes later the other woman emerged and pulled her up. They both faced the camera with their melted green faces and T-shirts that said JIMMY JOE CRAWFORD: THE BADDEST COWBOY ALIVE.

Next there was a cut to a grim-looking reporter in the casino, telling the whole world what Willy had let me in on ten minutes earlier. The DNA evidence that had been left at the scene, gathered from saliva samples, was unknown to forensic experts. The women were first believed to have been wearing masks, but experts studying the video believed that those were their real faces.

Mom walked in and Dad started screaming.

"WHAT IN THE UNIVERSE'S NAME DID YOU THINK YOU WERE DOING?"

He kept asking over and over again where her over-skin was. After what felt like the thirtieth time, she finally screamed back, "I THOUGHT YOU MISSED WHAT I USED TO LOOK LIKE!"

That shut him up because Mom never yells. Ever. Just then the governor came on TV to assure us that despite the rumors there was no evidence of an alien invasion. Dad finally lost it. He threw the remote at the TV so hard that it bounced off the screen and landed on the couch.

"All my careful plans," he mumbled. "All the years I've put into this."

Mom took several deep breaths, and she then went over to him and took him in her arms.

"I didn't know what Mother was up to," she said very softly. "She told me we had won a late dinner with Jimmy Joe. I didn't even know my overskin had come off until I saw the look on the bodyguard's face."

Dad said something into her sweater.

"What was that, darling?" Mom asked.

He lifted his head. "Where is she?"

"I'm right here. Quiet down before the neighbors hear you."

I jumped. Grandmother was right behind me. When I turned around, I jumped again. Her face had even more caverns in it than Mom's did and looked twice as melted.

I hurried over to Mom and scrunched down next to her. She put one of her arms around me.

"Stop blubbering," Grandmother said. "Everything is going as to plan. The Supreme High Council wants to raise the terror level in the humans, and sustain it for the best nutritional value possible."

"All of the militaries in the world are going to be on high alert from now on," Dad said.

She looked at him in disgust. Poor Dad. Grandpa had disappeared under mysterious circumstances. I wouldn't be at all surprised if Grandmother had something to do with it. Grandmother or not, I hated her.

"Do you think the feeble forces of this world concern us?" she was saying.

"They do have atomic weapons," I said.

"We are superior" was all she said to that. "Stan! Gerald!"

They came running in, their duffel bags packed and over their shoulders.

"We'll meet you at the Oasis." Then she pointed to me. "Before the rest are here, you will know what it means to hunt. As for you, husband to my daughter, any plans for you to sit on the Supreme High Council are foolhardy, and always have been."

Mom rose to her feet. "Now see here, Mother, there has been no one more loyal to the Home World. No one more willing to make sacrifices."

Grandmother smirked. "As I said, everything has gone exactly as planned."

She walked out the front door.

Stan and Gerald stood there looking embarrassed. Gerald shrugged, and the two of them followed her outside.

"What about her face?" I asked Mom.

"We can regenerate the overskin," she said. "I'm sure Stan will do all the driving until she has her human face back."

We slumped back on the floor next to Dad. He kissed Mom and said, "I forgot how beautiful you are."

Mom kissed him back, and then told him, "Darling, don't pay any attention to what Mother said. You deserve to be on the Council. The others will see to it."

He shook his head. "Earth has made us both too soft. She's right. Maybe we've just been tools for the Home World." He passed his hand over his face. For a moment I was afraid that he was going to cry. "Anyway, they're going to need people to run the snow parks." He turned to me. "Mom's got to try skiing. Don't you think, Deborah?"

Grandmother had just taken a knife and slashed my Dad's dreams to shreds. We were survivors, though. Snow park manager? Why not? A job like that had to be better than being the footstool of Our Most Supreme Imperial High Matriarch.

Chapter Twelve

The Oasis

Before we left the house, we hid all our equipment, along with mementos like my family's Home World picture. We had cabinets within cabinets and vaults beneath the garage. Even if the FBI searched our house while we were gone, it was doubtful they'd find anything.

Mom told me her new overskin would grow back in a jiffy, and she'd look like her old self again, at least for a little while. After the invasion, we'd all have to use Grandmother's beauty treatment to restore Home World looks. Ugh. One more thing I was going to have to get used to.

Finally, we were in the Impala, cloaking system in operation, flying south down the I-5. Mom piloted. Dad was in the passenger seat working on a budget projection.

"I don't know why you're bothering with all of that," Mom was saying. "Your boss isn't going to be worried about your being late with the budget forecast while he's being devoured."

"My company pays me for a service," he said, "and I'm providing it. Besides, didn't we just waste an hour dropping those silly pink bags of yours on your customers' front steps?"

"My customers will at least get a chance to use the products," Mom retorted.

I closed my eyes. They were going to bicker all the way to Las Vegas. The Oasis was seventy miles east of Vegas, a place so close to Area 51 we could spit on it. If the military caught us, they'd be glad to take us to the secret base and dissect us. Mom had said that Grandmother claimed it was the safest place we could go because they wouldn't be looking for us right under their noses.

I almost didn't care if we were found or not. I took the box with the chocolate kiss out of my pocket. I decided to eat the candy and confess everything. There might not be another time once we got to the motel.

"Mom, Dad," I said, "there's something I need to tell you, and it's not going to be easy."

Dad looked up from his paperwork. Mom gave me a quick glance in the rearview mirror.

"What is it, Deborah?" she asked.

I took a big breath, showed them the kiss on my outstretched palm, and then bit off the pointy part at the top.

My parents' tentacles shot to the roof.

"Dbkrrrsh!" they both cried at once. Mom almost lost control of the Impala.

"See," I said after I swallowed. "Still alive. I've been eating human food for about a month. It's delicious, and I've never felt better."

"Deborah, how could you do this to us?" Mom said.

"Can't we just conquer and subjugate," I asked, "and not feed?"

"She's found out the truth, George," Mom cried.

I needed a few moments before I realized what she meant.

"You lied to me!" I exclaimed.

"We didn't want you to be tempted," Dad said, more severely than I liked. "Feeding defines us. It's who we are as a species. It's our religion, our culture, our life."

"Then I don't want to be a part of our culture," I said. "I want to eat Whoppers and not the people I care about." I thought about Alicia's shiny tinsel smile. "I'm not even sure I want to eat people I don't like."

That made Dad even more furious.

"What on Earth are you thinking, Deborah? Humans kill each other all the time. Think about all of their wars. They're no different than us. If they could eat each other easily, they would."

I crossed my arms and looked down on the line of cars below us. My parents were total creeps.

Mom drove on in silence. About twenty minutes later, she turned on the radio and searched for a news station and found a talk show.

"I believe there's been a conspiracy since Roswell in 1947," a young man was saying.

She changed stations. Agent Mackenzie was in the middle of an interview. "We have found seventeen families who were at the Lucky Nugget on November twenty-third and who also live in the Sacramento area."

There was static, and I couldn't hear the reporter's question. Then the reception cleared for her answer.

"We are not releasing any names at this point."

Mom switched off the radio. "They're looking for us," she said.

Dad needed to stop in Bakersfield to mail in his reports. As we left the freeway and headed east, we floated by the burger joints. McDonald's, Jack in the Box, Burger King, Wendy's . . . I'd wanted to try them all and do a taste comparison and nutrition analysis for my science project, but now that idea was ruined. I'd never even get to try a filet mignon.

Just outside of Bakersfield we landed in secret and turned off the cloaking device so we could drive into town. Mom put a scarf around her head to hide her face from people in the other cars. Her humanlike skin had already grown about a third of the way up her neck and down from her hairline. The new skin was pink and shiny, kind of like a baby's, but the effect with her green wrinkly real skin was more unnerving than seeing her *au natural*.

Mom asked Dad to pick up copies of the *Los Angeles Times* and *San Francisco Chronicle* while he mailed his package. He took over piloting when he came back from the post office, and she riffled through the newspapers for the next hour.

As she turned the pages, she began to guilt trip me about my revelation. She'd been seething since I'd spilled the beans, and now I was finally going to get it.

"I don't know where your father and I went wrong raising you. We tried to teach you values, and what happens? You eat like a human." The way she said the word "human" made it sound like a word you wouldn't say in polite company. "If word of this gets out, the House of

Mpfld will be disgraced."

"You're not to breathe a word of this to anyone, you understand, young lady?" Dad piped in.

I hate how parents back each other up.

"You lied to me," I said.

"We were trying to make life easier for you," Dad said.

As if that justified it. They kept harping at me, demanding I promise the next meal I ate wouldn't come from a cow. I tuned them out the best I could. I kept my thoughts on Willy, his cape and long black fingernails during Halloween, and how much he'd improved in math. I missed him and hated leaving on this trip without saying good-bye. If my parents decided to disown me, maybe his parents would adopt me, but would that make him my brother, then? I didn't know if that would be weird or not.

The closer we got to the Oasis, the more agitated I felt. I wasn't looking forward to spending time with Grandmother in the boondocks. Of all the creeps I was related to, she was the creepiest.

A short while later, Mom folded the newspapers. "There's only speculation about the murders. They have nothing solid," she said, "but there is a nice article in the *Times* about patio furniture."

Finally I had something to say. "Maybe we're panicking for no reason. People go away on vacation. There's no reason for them to suspect us any more than the other sixteen families."

Dad looked at me sternly again.

"Because of your mother's behavior at the Lucky Nugget, Agent Mackenzie is going to remember us," he said. "No, they want us. The police are suppressing the news so the public doesn't get even more alarmed."

Mom looked at the clock nervously and changed the subject. "I told Mother we'd be there by seven."

As the hours wore on, I felt more and more alone in the backseat. An uncomfortable silence filled the car. I figured I'd better finish the kiss before we got to the motel because there was a very good chance I wasn't ever going to taste chocolate again. Dad glanced back at me as I nibbled on it, bewilderment on his face. I could almost hear him ask himself, "Where has my little cannibal gone?"

As we passed over Las Vegas, I peered down. The neon signs weren't glowing because it wasn't dark yet, but the Eiffel Tower and the pyramid were easy to spot.

The metropolis spread like a giant medusa dotted with the turquoise eyes of swimming pools, but finally the housing developments ended and desert emerged again. We followed the highway for a while and then turned off onto a small road we could barely see in the twilight. After a few miles, Dad lowered the Impala and we gently hit the asphalt. The road headed toward some low hills that looked like they had been molded in dried clay.

Dad turned onto a dirt road. The sky was dark now, and every few hundred yards a jackrabbit ran across the beam of our headlights. Just when I was wondering if we were in Utah yet, we drove beneath a sign with faded letters that said THE OASIS.

The motel consisted of five cottonwood trees and a row of dilapidated rooms. The Hummer was parked in front of the building. A sign that said OFFICE dangled vertically on one nail, and light showed through the dirty windows.

Grandmother walked outside before Dad had a chance to turn off the motor. When we got out, she greeted us with "You're late."

Mom looked at her watch. "Only by twenty minutes," she said.

A soft hum was coming through the open door of the office. Grandmother turned and led us inside. The whole room was full of blinking white and yellow lights, and seven monitors displayed different places around the planet. I stopped and watched a crowd of people jamming into a subway on the monitor labeled TOKYO, but then Mom grabbed me by the elbow and ushered me through another door that led to a back room.

The pink Naugahyde couch, the tray tables set around the room, and the picture of President Kennedy hanging lopsided on the wall all looked like they'd been there since 1962. Mom pushed me down on the couch, and she, Dad, and Grandmother towered over me.

"Where are Stan and Gerald?" I asked. I tried to smile but gave up when I saw their scowls. I remembered the Home World ritual my parents had frightened me with when I was little that required rebellious children to be eaten.

Grandmother scrutinized me. Her overskin had grown back faster than Mom's. Only her nose remained furrowed and green.

"When do you turn twelve?" Grandmother asked me.

"January fourteenth," I said. "In two weeks."

"We will have the purgation then," she announced, "and, as soon as it's over, we'll head back to Prattville."

"What's a purgation?" I asked.

No one answered me. Grandmother walked into the front office. Dad followed her. A few seconds later the front door slammed.

Even though Mom was a creep, I felt sorry for her. "Grandmother shouldn't talk to you that way," I said, and then I took a deep breath. "Are you and Dad ever going to forgive me?"

"Yes, of course," Mom said. "But you've got to live by the rules we set down for you."

I nodded reluctantly. "Mom, what's a purgation?"

"I can't tell you," she said. "I can only say that by going through it, you'll let go of Deborah Jones and become who you really are underneath."

I didn't like the sound of that one bit. Dad came back in, and then we followed him to our room. The temperature was dropping by the minute. The beds were old and the mattresses were lumpy, but there was a down sleeping bag on each one. Even with the cold seeping in, we'd be warm, but still I shivered from fear. What was going to happen to me?

Dad started snoring immediately. I stared up through the broken window. So many stars. I looked toward the horizon at the zigzag of Cassiopeia's crown. Somewhere near the fourth star was the home I'd never known.

This day had been the longest of my life. My eyes closed, and I dropped into a dreamless sleep.

The next morning I found everyone gathered around a TV set in the back room of the office. A morning news anchor was interviewing Agent Mackenzie. Even though she was after us, there was something about her I liked. I let myself daydream for a moment that if snowboarding didn't work out, I could work for the FBI.

"There has never been any alien DNA," she was saying. "There was some inconclusive evidence and somehow all of this mushroomed into an urban legend."

Grandmother turned off the TV.

"She's a clever one, isn't she?" she said.

I was really confused. "What's an urban legend?" I asked.

As usual, I was ignored.

Chapter Thirteen

Don't Be Too Afraid

"For the last time, it's *Hrthr-vtck*," Stan said. A few days had passed, and he was trying to teach me the right way to greet Our Most Supreme Imperial High Matriarch (and Queen of the Nine Planets, soon to be ten). "Put your tongue at the top of your mouth, vibrate it against your teeth, and then bring the back of your tongue up against your throat."

He said that the invading forces would mistake me for a *nklbkb*, one of the slaves that mopped up after the feeding parties. The only food they got was leftovers.

Because of my disgraceful pronunciation of our language, Stan took it upon himself to tutor me. This was our second lesson, and I was not doing well. As I tried once again to copy him, I managed to spit on his face.

Stan wiped his cheek.

"You spit on your hands, not on the other person's face, to be polite. If you do this when you're introduced to Her Majesty, she'll probably have your whole family turned into *nklbkbs*."

Like I really needed something else to worry about.

"I've always got *A*s in English," I said.

Stan wasn't impressed. After a half dozen more failed attempts, he shook his head and said, "We're not getting anywhere with this. We'll try again tomorrow." He stood up and stretched. "I've got to get back to the purgurator anyway."

I sighed and slumped down in my chair after he left the office. My parents continued to refuse to tell me what was going to happen during my purgation. All I knew was that Stan and Gerald were working in Room Five building my "birthday gift," and I didn't have a clue as to what it was.

My family kept following the news about the murders. Everyone else from the Lucky Nugget had been contacted and cleared, but Agent Mackenzie said there was one family that had disappeared. She didn't say our names, but it was us, the Joneses from Prattville.

I missed Willy through all of this. My parents wouldn't let me contact him: no IM nor e-mail, no phone calls, and definitely no letters. Mom said it was time to let him go. If he were a Home Worlder, he'd be going through his purgation, too, and we wouldn't have been allowed to be friends anymore.

Being surrounded by an alien culture, my native culture, made my life in Prattville seem like a dream. I had my own room now, and when I had the chance, I'd go there, wrap the sleeping bag around me, take out the homework that Mr. Bartlett had given me for the break, and plot points on a graph or find angles of isosceles triangles just to feel normal again. I also practiced my clarinet a lot, but when I did I kept thinking of the sound of Willy's sax playing "My Favorite Things."

As soon as I finished purgurating, all of us but Gerald would go back to Prattville to help coordinate the invasion. Our ships would send down special microwaves to disrupt all of Earth's nuclear weapons. We wanted to be in charge of any destruction that might happen.

Stan and Gerald were busy day and night, working on the purgurator and inspecting and testing the relay devices we'd need for the invasion on the seventeenth, three days after my birthday. Dad said the two of them were some of the very best technicians the Home World had, and that's why they were chosen to come to Earth with Grandmother. Gerald was so busy, in fact, that I hardly ever saw him, which was fine with me because I can't tell you how awkward I felt when I was near him.

I really wanted to do well with my debut in Home World society, so I worked hard on my pronunciation. Speaking our language sure wasn't like snowboarding. It was full of clicks and grunts, and if you did one just too low or too high you could risk bringing shame to your family for generations to come. "Loosen up," I said to myself, but I bit my tongue instead, three times in one lesson.

When I wasn't practicing disgusting guttural sounds, I had to study some data orbs that Grandmother gave me about the history of why my family was on top of the social heap and the *nklbkbs* weren't. It all had to do with wars thousands of years ago. As I listened to the tapes, it didn't seem fair to me that only ten percent of us had privileges like full stomachs just because our ancestors were able to eat their ancestors into submission. But I didn't say anything because no one wanted to hear what I thought.

My biggest problem of all, though, was that I was starving again. Eating human food had sped up my metabolism. I was even tempted to eat a jackrabbit or two just to curb my hunger pangs, but somebody was always watching me.

Whenever my stomachs growled, Grandmother gave me weird looks that made me uncomfortable. One night in the office, right before I was going to turn in, they gurgled especially loudly. Grandmother looked up from the charts she was studying. Her and Mom's faces had grown back, but Grandmother's scarlike wrinkles were even deeper now. "You'll be ready," she said in a spooky tone.

Had Mom told her about what I'd been eating? Had she figured out why I was always hungry?

I told everyone good night. I walked along the cracked concrete, and the cold seeped through my sweat-shirt and pajama bottoms. Waves of panic washed over me and chilled me even more.

What would I be ready for? Did Grandmother have some punishment picked out for me, a birthday surprise to teach me a lesson? Or was something else going to happen? I stared at the dark ceiling. I didn't need to sleep to have nightmares.

*

On the eve of my birthday, Dad and I climbed one of the hills behind the motel.

"The desert seems to go on forever," I said when we got to the top. I tried not to think of what the lizard on the rock next to us might taste like. I was almost as hungry as I was before I fed on those poor college kids.

"Space feels a lot like this," Dad said, once he caught his breath. He needed to get more exercise.

Just then we heard a jet passing overhead. I squinted and looked up and saw the sun reflecting off the plane's surface. The roar was several miles behind and seemed like it chased the plane across the sky.

"Do you think they know we're out there?" I asked Dad.

"I can only guess," he said, "but I know even ordinary people on Earth sense they can't be the only life in the universe. Your grandmother thinks the governments of Earth suspect our presence here, but when it comes down to it, it really doesn't matter because . . ."

I tuned out what he was saying. We were superior. What else was new? I started to think about Willy again. "My Favorite Things" was stuck in my head.

"Don't be too afraid tomorrow," Dad said, and this brought me right smack back into the middle of Nevada.

"What was that?"

"During your purgation. Don't let your fears take control. It would have been impossible for you to even get a taste of what you'll be going through, even if we had let you hunt on Halloween."

"A taste of what?" I asked.

"Your first kill completely on your own."

I swallowed hard, but I wanted to find out as much as I could about what I had to go through. "The policeman didn't count?"

Dad squinted, and a trickle of sweat leaked under his hat, which was twitching. He put his arm around my shoulder and drew me close. "You were in no danger, were you?"

"He didn't fight back," I said. The purgation was just a simulation, right? Why should I be afraid of a simulation? "Dad, there's no way anything made from a hologram or whatever they're rigging in Room Five could hurt me."

I thought I sounded very logical, very calm.

"Deborah, this is hard to explain. The purgurator creates more than a simulation. The thing that Gerald and Stan are building is an exact match to what boys and girls all over the Home World enter on their twelfth birthdays. It's not a hologram. It takes you to another dimension, another time, when the mastery of our home was still being determined. And if you don't pass the test, you won't be allowed to come back out."

It was a good thing his arm was around me because my knees buckled when he said that. "You're as smart as any kid from the Home World, Dbkrrrsh. Your reflexes are quick, and you have a lot of spirit. These things will help you succeed."

He said that my chances were excellent, and the fact I was so hungry would be a huge benefit and would make me fight like a champion.

"Mom and I decided that the two of us should have this little talk, even though we're technically breaking the rules." Dad said. He was still holding me. "The purgation is a secret that grown-ups keep from children. Once you go through yours, you never talk about it."

I would have stolen the Impala in the middle of the night and run away, if only I knew how to drive.

Chapter Fourteen

Purgation

There was a thundershower the night before my birthday. I lay in my sleeping bag and watched the windows light up and counted until I heard the rolls of thunder. Somehow in the middle of this, I fell asleep, but it seemed like only minutes had passed when Mom woke me.

I rolled over and put the pillow over my head. I felt her standing above me, so I forced myself to reach for the pile of clothes I'd left by the mattress.

"You won't need those, sweetie," she said.

"I don't have to do this thing naked, do I?" I asked with my head still under the pillow.

"Of course not," she said.

I forced myself to sit up. Mom was holding out something similar to the silver jumpsuits we'd all been wearing. This outfit, though, was all black and had feet like the pajamas I wore when I was little.

I took the suit. It was surprisingly light, and there were rubberlike soles on the bottom of the feet, good for traction.

"Put it on," she said, and then she gave me a sad smile. I was ready to give her the eye roll, but instead she just walked outside. I didn't even get a kiss. I felt cheated.

I slipped on the suit. I kept my underwear on, though I wasn't sure if I was breaking some sort of taboo by being partially clad in an Earth garment.

When I stepped outside, gray clouds lay low on the hills, and the whole desert had a silver cast from the rain.

"It's so beautiful," I said, thinking I was talking to myself.

"A good sign."

I turned around. Gerald was standing next to my parents. He was holding a necklace, a long gold chain with a small silver rock dangling at the end of it.

"For good luck," Gerald told me as he leaned over and put it over my head. For a moment, I was afraid he might kiss me. That was the last thing I needed, but instead he whispered. "I can't help you any other way. Don't forget you have it."

"Thank you," I said, examining the rock.

"Tuck it in your suit," Mom said, "and stick your tentacles out all the way."

I looked at the rock again. The silver caught the light and sparkled, and it looked as if it was beginning to glow.

Dad squeezed my shoulder a little too hard. "We might as well get this over with," he said.

We walked down the concrete walk to Room Five, everyone's tentacles unfurled. The smell of the rain stimulated my appetite even more. I wasn't merely ravenous. I could have eaten a cow.

Dad knocked on the door. Stan opened it and smiled

at me. I'd finally mastered how to say "Hrthr-tck" without spraying him on my last lesson.

We followed Stan inside. I was shocked to see what they'd done to the motel room. A huge silver orb, pulsating with green lights, filled most of the room. I thought, *Can these guys build, or what? Two points for the home team*, but then a door slid open from the orb and Grandmother walked out. I was feeling almost confident, but one look from her and my spirits sunk as low as Death Valley.

"Everything is ready," she said. "Let's begin."

I leaned over and looked behind Grandmother. There was a sloping incline behind the door of the orb that led deep down into the ground. I could see only about ten feet; beyond that was pitch-black.

Mom and Dad were being good little soldiers. I wanted them to be gushing and sad. Wasn't this the perfect time for sentimentality, when their only child might be eaten by . . . by what?

I looked at Gerald. I thought perhaps he wanted to say something to me, but maybe it was only my imagination. I wouldn't have minded his finding another good luck token somewhere in the room just then—like maybe a gun.

Grandmother stepped aside. I waited for someone to at least say, "On your mark, get set, go!" but after about fifteen seconds I realized I had already had all the send-off I was going to get. I took my first step, and total darkness engulfed me. I felt like I was falling down a dark pit. I started to sing underneath my breath.

Happy birthday to me . . .

My heart felt like a dog's tail was thumping inside me.

I had no idea what to do. Just stand there? I was too afraid to move.

Finally, after a couple of minutes, a soft glow shimmered across the floor. I didn't know if this was a good thing or not, but it reminded me of the way the fog rises in the winter around Sacramento. I thought about the time my family had been caught in fog on the freeway and how quickly Dad had to slow down. I'd been on the edge of my seat, afraid we'd rear-end another car. I was feeling the exact same way now, my whole body afraid of what I couldn't see.

Happy birthday to me . . .

The air got thicker and stung my lungs. If I'd still been in Prattville, the weatherman would have declared a smog alert. Landforms slowly emerged in the distance through the haze.

In half a heartbeat, the fog disappeared and everything around me became intensely real. I was still in a desert, the land around me arid and stark, but I sure wasn't in Nevada anymore. There was no way wildflowers would ever grow in a place like this.

Happy birthday, dear Deborah . . .

A strong wind was blowing. My cheeks tingled from the cold, but the suit was keeping me warm. I started to feel a little better. I'd be able to move in a moment or two. I sensed that gravity was slightly heavier on Earth.

For good luck, I felt for the silver stone Gerald had given me and started to walk down a hill that fell off into a steep slope after the first few steps. The environment felt as if it was molding around me, responding to my body. The soles on the bottom of my suit were definitely designed for this place.

When I got to the bottom, I saw a single tall tree off in the distance. It was impossible to know how far, really. Should I walk to it? There might be a water source near the tree. The constant for life in the universe is the availability of water, but . . . a creature was out to get me, and I would have to fight. Wouldn't my going toward the tree be the exact thing it would expect me to do?

I scanned the immediate area and found a rock that looked like a big baked potato and would do for a shelter from the wind, and I sat down behind it. I was on the Home World. There were pictures of this desert on an old calendar my mom had back in my other home, the one on Cedar Street, two blocks from school, and a galaxy away. I was finally on the Home World.

I was going to need water, but for the short run I was okay. My tummies ached and were growling like crazy. Maybe I was being paranoid, but the noises sounded like a homing beam to whatever was out there. *Yoo-hoo, here I am, come and get me.*

I stayed planted for at least an hour until I knew I had to move or I'd fall asleep. I wondered how many kids did that, just froze until they became apple fritters to a hungry beast. I finally pushed myself up and started to jog toward the tree.

Once again my shoes impressed me. Somehow they counteracted the gravity just enough to make me feel like I was skimming over the surface. Once I got my stride, I ran faster than I ever had in my life. I was adapting to the bad air, too. I wouldn't have been surprised that whatever minerals were in the acrid smell might be nutrients, things my body longed for and needed to perform at its very best.

Food was on my mind, as always. *Essence*. The essence of another being's fear filling me as I fed. I remembered how a fully sentient, conscious being was so much more satisfying than even pork.

My tentacles were on full alert, the cilia flowing and receiving impulses. There was a cry in a canyon to the west. My instincts said to ignore it, that the sound came from a creature too small for me to worry about.

I was more awake than I'd ever been. I was absolutely terrified, but this other part of me was stirring. Where I was now, hearing the soft thud thud of my feet on the ground, feeling my tentacles waving freely above me, taking deep breaths of this rich air, was the only place I'd ever been. Memories of life on Earth were distant as a faded black-and-white photograph.

But then I thought of Dad.

Not everyone comes back.

I heard his voice in my head, and, zap, that old photograph turned into a big-screen full color DVD. I saw Willy, the way he looked on Halloween with his fangs and cape, his smile as we walked home from school together. If he survived the invasion, how was I going to explain that I was engaged to Gerald?

Just then I stopped running so suddenly I almost tumbled over my feet. I'd done the most stupid thing imaginable. How many kids never came back because they got lost? There could be more reasons for not returning other than losing a food fight.

I hadn't paid attention to where I was before I started out. I looked behind me. Which direction was the door? All the twisting red rock formations looked the same.

A whipping sound buzzed through the air to my left. I didn't have the time to scream before something yanked on my ankle, and then it felt as if it had been stung by a hive of yellow jackets. I fell flat on my face in the dirt. Slobbery wet panting accompanied a quick succession of short little jerks.

With each jerk I skidded backward on my belly. The pain throbbed up to my knee; I was sure I'd been poisoned. Was it going to end like this? So quickly?

I looked behind me but could only see a furry brown rope full of spiky golden burrs wrapped around my ankle.

Maybe I could reason with whatever was pulling me toward my death.

"You know, we don't have to be enemies," I called out. "Why don't we call a truce?"

A loud growl was my only answer. Silly Earth stuff like negotiating wasn't going to work.

Well, I wasn't going to give in without a fight. I had the reputation of my people to uphold. We were the biggest, baddest species in the galaxy, and I wasn't going to let them down. I braced myself for three more jerks, and then on the fourth I rolled over.

The next yank pulled me a longer distance than all of the others combined, but I managed to sit up. I saw nothing but four or five meters of the rope trailing in front of me. What was pulling me?

Yank.

I felt like Pinocchio being swallowed by the whale, and I imagined huge cavernous jaws. Pain seared up my leg. I looked around for a sharp rock, anything I could use to either cut the rope or defend myself. There was nothing, only sandy red dirt. I picked up a handful. Maybe I could throw it into the creature's eyes. If I could find them.

The idea was so ridiculous that I almost laughed. What was I? Some kind of sissy? I had six perfectly good tentacles each with three rows of sharply serrated teeth. I knew what I had to do. I had to do it fast, but it was going to hurt. A lot.

I had to sacrifice my favorite tentacle because it was in the front and I could throw it the farthest. It was pink, and I'd always thought it was kind of cute. With the next yank, I swung my head forward and pushed the tentacle out as far as it would go. Its mouth reached only a little past my foot.

I almost bit off my toe, but fortunately I missed and chopped the rope in two. I was free, but now there was a firestorm raging inside me. It felt like twenty burrs embedded in my tongue and gums of the pink tentacle. My other five tentacles screamed in sympathy, but the rope loosened and I was able to pull my foot away.

I've wanted a puppy ever since I was little. My parents always said no, for the usual reasons. I'd always told myself I'd never eat a dog, no matter how desperate I got. But now I was more than happy to break my rule. I'd have eaten an entire team of sled dogs from the Iditarod if they'd been on the other end of that rope.

The creature that rose from the dirt wasn't really a dog. If evolution on Earth had gone in a totally different direction and the dominant species was a sentient German shepherd that stood erect, had opposable thumbs, and slobbered, you might have an idea of what I was up against.

Only "it" wasn't an it. She was female and looked about my age. I got it then. The purgation was a reenactment of a ritual that had gone on long ago. The Dog People versus Us. The young on both sides were sacrificed to find out who would take control of the planet.

I'd wounded it, but only slightly. The "rope" was actually her tail, and the part that I hadn't bitten off was spinning around her head like a lasso, flicking orange blood in every direction.

She threw her tail again. The buzzing whirled toward my neck, but I squatted quickly enough for it to miss me. I scooted several steps backward, tears welling in my eyes. Both my pretty pink tentacle and my left leg felt like they were being held against a hot stove.

She growled something at me. From the look on her face, she could have been saying something like "Die, alien scum," only that's the title of our planetary anthem. I'm sure the gist was the same, though.

Still, I had five good tentacles, and all she had was a whipping cat-o'-nine tail, some incredibly sharp dagger-like claws, and huge fangs that she bared at me in a sinister smile. Plus all that slobber.

Full frontal attack, I thought? Take her by surprise with all of my teeth exposed and ready to rip? That had to be frightening, right? Or should I just say to heck with it and run?

She leaped in my direction, sailing through the distance between us like an Olympic long jumper. In a heartbeat she had wrapped her crummy tail around my tentacles as if she was tying them up into a bouquet.

How did we ever become the dominant species against the likes of her? She slobbered again and let me dangle while she pondered which part of me would be tastiest. My hands were free, but so what? She had arms over a meter long. I couldn't reach her eyes even if I could have poked them out with my fingers.

I took hold of Gerald's good luck charm and held it out so I could look at it one last time. Good-bye, Mother. Father. Willy. Gerald. I was never going to play the clarinet again or go to the mall or . . .

Suddenly the stone sparkled and grew warm in my hands, and a blinding ray of light blasted from it, straight at my enemy's eyes. Dog Girl had just enough time to whine, and then, zap, she let go of me and fell jerking to the ground. That's how we did it! We had technology on our side. That silver stone wasn't just a pretty souvenir from home. It was a tendrilizer. Dad told me about them once. They not only stunned the enemy; they marinated them in their own juices.

I landed on my feet. My wounds were worse than fire now, but instead of making me feel weak, they enraged me. I felt powerful, and I was very, very hungry.

Once I read about how Viking warriors went "berserk" during battle, crazed with the gore and the blood, utterly invincible. As I ripped her flesh, I became one with all who ever fed, and then there it was, the sweet taste of fear lodged in her muscles and organs. As I swallowed her last thoughts, I tasted her essence on my tongues.

When I was done, I rolled over. Her blood was already seeping down and blending into the soil of my world. Never before had I been truly sated. I was here on my beautiful world, and I never wanted to leave. I'd forgotten any thought of wanting to find the door back to

Nevada. I wanted to stay and be free and, when I was ready, to feed once again.

Light burst over me, and the aquamarine sky disappeared. Instead, I saw the bolts and the silver panels of the purgurator overhead, and once again I had the feeling I was being buried, this time in a metal egg.

No, I want to go back, I thought. *I don't want to be here in Nevada.*

The door swung open and everyone, including Grandmother, marched in applauding. (Every species in the galaxy does this to show pleasure for a performance. No one has figured out why.) I sat up, extremely out of sorts. "Why did you bring me back?" I yelled. "Why did I have to come back here?"

Mom and Dad beamed down at me, and I saw the little crinkles around their eyes. They were too old to understand what I was going through.

"Oh, I remember that feeling," Mom said. "I kicked and screamed all the way back from the Desolation Area. I pouted for days."

"Me, too," Dad said, as he squatted in front of me, checking me over. I wasn't hurting anymore, but I wanted the pain. I wanted to feel that real again, that alive. The experience was already beginning to fade. I didn't want it to end. I was still hungry. I needed to go back. Now.

I touched my pink tentacle. It felt fine. Then I reached for Gerald's necklace again. I looked at him. He understood. He'd go back without a second thought.

"Good job," Grandmother said. "I had my doubts about you, but you've surprised me. Do you think a hamburger could ever satisfy you again?"

So Grandmother knew I had violated our species' greatest taboo. I had to believe I'd earned my family's confidence in me again.

I stood up shakily and stepped backward, away from them, just as custom called for. By doing so I was telling them that I knew I was a hunter, no longer dependent on them, but someone who would defend all of them and our planet with my life.

"We got a planet to conquer," I said, and everyone spit.

Chapter Fifteen

Essence of Home

We didn't celebrate my birthday with cake and ice cream, of course. The tendrilizer was the only present I received. Now that I was an adult, I'd never celebrate a birthday again. What I did get was the satisfaction of knowing I hadn't let my parents down, and that I finally knew I was not Deborah Jones, but Dbkrrrsh of the House of Mpfld, the Home World's oldest and most glorious family.

Today, Saturday, January 14, my twelfth and last birthday, could not have come at a better time. In three short days the skies would fill with the hot metallic glow of hundreds of airships of all sizes. My species would descend and Earth would finally be ours, thanks to Mom, Dad, and me.

Almost as great, we still had time to get home for Math Champs, which would be taking place on the evening of the seventeenth, just hours before our ships planned to land. I planned to do some vanquishing myself before planet Earth met the same fate. Alicia was dead meat, in more ways than one.

That night was also the film festival. I hoped Willy and his family would have a good time at it, since it would be the last time they were ever going to have fun.

Get a grip, I thought. *Grandmother is right. What is friendship compared to essence?*

By the time I changed back into my sweatshirt and jeans and stepped outside from my room, Mom was putting a box into the trunk of the Impala. The air in Nevada was disgustingly clean and fresh, and I longed for the sulfuric air of the Desolation Area.

"We're going home?" I asked, walking to the car.

"We're leaving first thing tomorrow morning," Mom said. "George is calling Agent Mackenzie as we speak."

"Oh," I said, surprised Dad had contacted her.

Mom closed the trunk. "We thought we'd be proactive and tell her we were on vacation and hadn't followed the story in the news. We don't want to suddenly appear out of nowhere and have the FBI snooping around our house, so we're inviting Agents Mackenzie and Samuelson to visit on Monday night to reassure them we're safe and sound, and to help divert any suspicions they might still have. Our equipment is locked up tight. They won't find a thing."

Even if they did, I thought, who cared? It would be Invasion Eve and we could eat them.

"I'll go pack," I said.

Mom grabbed my hand before I turned to go. Giving it a squeeze, she said, "I want you to know how proud I am of you. Even your grandmother was impressed. Things are looking up."

"Thanks," I said. "But Mom, I'm starving even more than before I ate Dog Girl."

She nodded. "That's the effect of the purgation, plus I'm sure Earth food played havoc with your metabolism. Three days, Deborah. Only three days left."

Before we left Nevada, we took a short side trip and hovered over Hoover Dam for a little while. We were all impressed, and Dad reminded me that we were going to definitely keep some of the more capable and talented humans alive to work for us.

When we got home Sunday night, the three of us were so tired we went right to bed. Grandmother and Stan drove the Hummer and must have arrived in the wee hours of Monday morning because they were there when I woke up.

How strange it was to be back in a neighborhood with row upon row of identical houses with the same squares of grassy lawn in front. Kids were walking to school instead of having to fight for their lives. Later in the day, pizza delivery vans would slow to maneuver around their ball games in the street. Dinner could be delivered straight to the door.

Tomorrow I'd be truly home for the first time in my life. I'd never have to hide anything again. I'd be who I really was, tentacles free, no longer the kid different from everyone else. There would be plenty of Home World kids my age to be with. My peers would all have gone through their purgation, though. I wasn't sure if we'd be allowed to hang out.

Before the two agents arrived Monday evening, Mom baked cookies. Our house smelled like the Pillsbury

Doughboy had come for a visit.

Right off the bat, Agent Samuelson grabbed three cookies. I'm sure Agent Mackenzie watched what she ate because she didn't touch them. The two of them looked around for a little while and seemed satisfied with our story. They called the Oasis, and Gerald pretended to be the manager and said that yes, indeed, we'd vacationed there.

Before they left, Mom said, "Agent Mackenzie, thank you again for your kindness at the casino."

"It was the least I could do," she said. "I have a sister who has a similar problem, so I felt a connection with you."

As they drove off, Grandmother, who actually had put on some of Mom's lipstick for the visit, said, "I just bet. Did you see how she kept looking at the Impala? Tomorrow night can't happen soon enough."

It was all I could do to hold in my tentacles while the agents were in the house. The smell of the cookies egged on my appetite for essence. When the agents finally left, the moment we shut our front door, all six exploded out of my head.

"Can't I do a little terrorizing tonight, please?" I begged.

I could still taste Dog Girl's fear, and I wanted more of the same, to feel fear through my skin, to taste it in the air. I wasn't going to be picky. I didn't care whose fear it was. I just wanted to smell it around me.

"Patience," Mom said.

Dad winked at me. "I knew you'd be a go-getter from the time you were born," he said.

I thought about our conversation the night before my

purgation and how Dad always looked out for me. He understood me, maybe even better than Mom. I was hungry, but I was lucky. I pulled my tentacles in. I could wait.

Before I left for school Tuesday morning, I helped to change the sheets, and I cleaned the mirror in the bathroom. Who knew who would be spending the night with us? I'm sure my parents were daydreaming about hosting a Supreme High Council member or two.

I, on the other hand, was daydreaming about seeing Willy again. This would be my last day to be a sixth grader, the last day I'd have to put up with Mr. Bartlett. I had Math Champs to look forward to that evening, and then the horror fest. Between now and then, I was going to make the best of it.

I decided to ride my bike to school. I put on my cap to be on the safe side in case my tentacles popped again. The morning was crisp, so it felt good covering my head.

When I got to school, there were ten minutes left before the first bell rang. I locked my bike and hurried to the playground to find Willy. Alicia was playing tetherball. There was going to be plenty of time to toy with her later, so I ignored her.

Amanda came hopping up on her jump rope.

"You're back," she said.

Duh, I thought, but I smiled anyway, trying to be compassionate. She might be someone's dinner in the not-too-far-distant future. "Yeah, we had an extended vacation."

Willy was standing by the basketball courts. "Hey," I shouted, and waved big so he could see me.

Willy turned around and waved. Oh, to be an alien girl with a crush on an Earth boy. It was almost like Romeo and Juliet, except this time Juliet got to party after Romeo died.

Willy ran into the court, intercepted the ball, and tried to make a hook shot. The ball missed by a mile.

"He's going with Alicia," Amanda said.

I almost asked, "Where are they going?" but then I realized what she meant.

This wasn't making any sense. I'd only been gone two weeks, and somehow she'd completely turned her feelings around *again* and had gone all the way to girlfriend status?

"But Alicia told me she thinks Willy is a loser," I said, shaking my head.

"Not anymore," Amanda told me, and then jumped away from me. "He's on the Math Champs team now."

Willy ran up to me.

"Deborah, it's great to see you. You'll never guess what?"

"What?" I said.

The whole playground went blurry. The bell rang, and I quickly wiped my red tears with my sleeve. I wasn't going to blow my cover this late in the game. No one was *ever* going to see me cry again. These were going to be the very last tears I'd shed for the rest of my life.

"Are you getting pink eye?" Willy asked.

"No," I said. "Something must be in the air."

"Deborah, you'll never guess what? Chen moved to Vallejo over vacation. I won a place on the math team. I beat everyone. Even in algebra."

Once again I felt myself cornered. This meant Willy

and Alicia had been studying together. Dog Girl's and Alicia's faces blurred into each other. The only thing I was capable of doing at that moment was to attack.

"I can't believe that," I said.

Willy's smile melted. "Thanks for nothing," he said, and turned around and walked off.

Willy ignored me the whole time our class waited for Mr. Bartlett to come from the teachers' room. Alicia stood three kids in front of me. She whispered something to Amanda. They giggled, and then Alicia gave me this smirky look.

Mr. Bartlett put his hand on my shoulder, and I jumped. "Deborah has decided to return just in the nick of time," he said, and then in a sarcastic voice added, "Isn't this wonderful, class?"

No one said anything, but Jenny, a new girl who'd come right before Thanksgiving, did give me a little hello smile. I put her on the vegetable list to replace Chen. She was the only one I wouldn't eat out of the lot of them.

Everything was exactly the same: roll, pledge, current events, reading, math. Math was so incredibly stupid. Any *nmchklt* could do it in a second.

I didn't need to go to school anymore. My superiority became clearer and clearer to me as the minutes wore on. My vanquishing of Dog Girl had proven this. All of these kids put together couldn't have defeated her.

Willy had a spiteful look and played with the pens in his desk every chance he got. Mr. Bartlett had his name on the board with a checkmark before morning recess. Alicia and Amanda kept giggling. I suffered through the rest of the morning, and then lunch. At last, at 12:30 the band kids were excused.

I looked forward to band as another way to prove my superiority. I could play every piece of music forward and backward by now, and I never squeaked on the high notes anymore. The rest of the clarinet section would be left in the dust.

Mr. Spencer broke out in a big smile when I walked in the room. I started to walk to my old seat, but he said, "Ah, Deborah. I'm afraid that's Alicia's place now. Would you mind being third chair? Tony's absent today."

Alicia? In my seat? I was being sent to the land of the low notes?

"But Mr. Spencer," I started to protest.

"Thanks, Deborah," he said, not listening, and told one of the drummers to spit out his gum. I made a mental note: *Mr. Spencer = meat list.*

Alicia watched me the whole time, and a sliver of her silvery teeth gleamed. It would be so sweet to attack her. Just reach over with a tentacle and snap . . .

As we played, I caught the band's reflection from the practice room's window. Willy sat in the row behind me, staring at his sheet music like it was the most fascinating comic book ever written.

Mr. Spencer tapped his baton on his stand and raised it over his head. We tuned our instruments and started to play a John Philip Sousa march. I did my part perfectly, but the whole time "Die, Alien Scum" played inside my head.

Later, Mr. Bartlett kept Alicia, Willy, and me while the rest of the class went to P.E.

"Tonight's the night," he said. "Deborah, Alicia, I would suggest that you not disappoint me. You would not enjoy the consequences."

"Then why is Willy on the team?" I asked.

I felt Willy seethe beside me.

"I've asked myself that question fifty times since Chen moved away," Mr. Bartlett said. "But somehow Willy qualified over the other students, and I could not figure out how he cheated."

"You're telling me that Willy Logan beat out all the other kids?" I asked incredulously.

Alicia nudged closer to Willy so that her arm touched his. What in the name of purgation was this about?

"You're being so mean to Willy," she taunted.

"You told me Willy was a loser because his family lost the case," I sniped back.

Alicia's eyes narrowed. "You were the one who said that, Deborah."

I might be mean. Some might even consider me a murderer. But I didn't tell lies like Alicia Henderson.

After school I found Grandmother standing by the flagpole talking to Margie, waiting to take me home in the Hummer. As soon as Grandmother saw me, she scanned me head to toe to see if I'd been corrupted by one day of school. It ticked me off that she still didn't trust me. I was more ready for the invasion than ever. Was I going to pay for the sins of chocolate and fast food forever?

When I got close enough, Margie gave me a big hug.

"Oh, Deborah, we've missed you." Then she saw Willy and called out, "Oh, there's Willy. Over here."

She turned back to Grandmother and me. "Willy has a dentist appointment this afternoon, and then we have to get ready for both Math Champs and the horror festival.

My husband's been working all day at the theater, but he's coming back for Willy's big night."

Willy walked up lugging his saxophone.

"Aren't you thrilled Deborah's back?" Margie asked. Willy just looked at the ground. Margie sensed something was wrong and looked slightly stressed. "Hey, I've got an idea. Why don't we take Deborah along with us tonight to the horror festival after the math contest?"

"But . . . ," Willy and I said at the same time.

"Do you think her parents would mind, Peggy?" Margie asked Grandmother. "We're taking Alicia along, and I'm sure the three of them would have lots of fun."

Deep inside my head my tentacles felt like Jell-O. Dog Girl wanted to come up. I had to say something, or I really was going to explode. "But Alicia's family hates your family."

"Oh, we got all of that worked out. Our lawyer appealed, and to make a long story short, we compromised. Willy can dress any way he likes for the last week of October. And, in the process, we found out our families do have a lot in common."

Was Alicia Willy's girlfriend because their parents were getting along? Or was it his new math skills?

I was sure Grandmother was going to tell Margie that we had other plans, but calculations passed over her face as she hatched a new idea.

"Deborah should go and spend time with her friends," Grandmother said. "I think it's a wonderful idea."

"We'll take her right from Math Champs, then," Margie said, giving Willy a look that said "Snap out of it." "Deborah, would you wear that great costume you wore for the wedding?"

By the time we climbed into the Hummer, I was so angry I didn't care that it was Grandmother I was talking to. "No way can I go to that horror festival tonight. Don't I have responsibilities or something for this invasion?"

Grandmother ignored my rudeness. She chuckled deviously. "You'll go, and when Our Most Supreme Imperial High Matriarch arrives, our family will escort her to the theater to feed." Her eyes grew narrow with ambition and glory. "Think of all of those people in the theater, already tenderized with fear. And then you'll show her your math crown."

"Grandmother, you're telling me that the most powerful woman in the galaxy is going to be impressed that I won a grammar school math competition?"

Grandmother gave a rare smile. "She's been keeping track of you, Dbkrrrsh. Your mother explained that it's customary to snack during the invasion, even if you're full, didn't she?"

"I can't wait," I said, thinking of Alicia.

Grandmother started the Hummer.

"Since you have grown up on Earth, it is important that you prove your loyalty so no one from home doubts which side you're on," she said. "It's important to the Supreme High Council, your future, and your parents' careers."

I told her of my plans for Alicia.

"That's a good start," Grandmother said. "But I think they'll expect more. If, for example, you choose to kill your best friend as well."

A lump rose in my throat as her implication became clear. I was back to exactly where I had been at Thanksgiving.

"But Willy's not my best friend anymore," I said weakly.

Grandmother pulled out of the parking lot. "That will make things a lot easier for you, won't it?"

I closed my eyes and tried to drum up the feeling of essence flooding my body, Willy's essence, his fear and betrayal that would make him delicious to devour.

"Duty and career," I whispered all the way home. I knew I could kill him, despite the red tear I wiped from my face.

Chapter Sixteen

Math Champ

I have to say one thing about my parents: they really do care about me. Despite how busy they were double-checking the relays and communications, and making sure that the travel itinerary for Our Most Supreme Imperial High Matriarch was to her liking (she kept changing her mind, now she wanted to go to Disney World, not Disneyland), they still found time to come to Math Champs.

We left Stan at our house. He was going to call Dad on his cell phone if there were any emergencies, but none were anticipated. When we got to school, we found the cafeteria decorated with blue and white balloons, our school colors, and math activities for each grade level covered the tables. Punch and cookies were being sold by the PTA, and the cafeteria buzzed with kids estimating beans in a jar or finding out how long things were in units of gummy worms. Parents chatted pleasantly around the perimeter or wandered in and out among the tables. Up on the stage, I saw the Math Champ Crown sitting on a desk draped with a royal blue tablecloth.

We weren't there ten minutes when Mr. Bartlett announced the sixth grade Math Champs contest was about to begin. Just then, Margie, Fred, and Willy came in a little flustered. His parents had a lot on their hands tonight, too, with the horror festival just hours away.

What a horror fest it was going to be, too.

In a jiffy all the games were cleared off the tables, and everyone found a seat. Twelve sixth graders walked onto the stage. I took my place, making sure I sat *between* Alicia and Willy.

The team competition took place for the first half hour. Problems were displayed on a screen and each team had to work together on answers. The kids in Mr. Carroll's class didn't correctly convert decimals to fractions on the first round. Mrs. Thomas's class flubbed a long division problem that had dividends and divisors in the hundred thousands. It came down to Mrs. Jacobs's class and ours.

Mr. Bartlett displayed this problem:

Joe had some money to spend. He spent half of it on new CDs. He spent 5 dollars at the video arcade. He spent half of his remaining money on comic books. Now he has 10 dollars left. How much did he start with?

Good old mathematical reasoning.

Ten seconds later, Sarah Gunderson from Mrs. Jacobs's class shouted out, "Forty-five!"

Never one to mince words, Mr. Bartlett announced, "You are absolutely wrong."

I decided to let the other two actually earn the win, and to my surprise, it was Willy, not Alicia, who figured out the right answer.

"He had fifty dollars to begin with," he announced.

For the twelfth year in a row, Mr. Bartlett's class had

kept the team competition trophy. The audience cheered as Mr. Bartlett handed it to Alicia, but he gave me the weirdest smile while he did so. I assumed it was because the last round was coming, and we both knew the Math Champ Crown belonged to me.

"Good luck, Deborah," he said, and then he sneezed. But it seemed to me more of a fake sneeze and my name almost sounded like "Dbkrrrsh."

Mr. Bartlett called Alicia's name first, and she picked one of the sealed envelopes that lay on his podium. She walked to the overhead, and announced, "Mathematical reasoning," to the audience. Luck of the draw, two word problems in a row.

She then read:

One train left Prattville on the B&O Railroad at 3 o'clock traveling to Bakersfield, 300 miles away, at 60 miles an hour. Another train left Prattville on the B&O Railroad for Bakersfield at 4 o'clock traveling at 80 miles an hour. What time did the two trains arrive, and which one arrived first?

Alicia grabbed the overhead pen and started to draw a diagram, but then she stopped and smiled. "The first train arrived in Bakersfield at eight. The second train could never get there because there is only one track. This is a trick question."

She sat down and was beaming. I hadn't noticed before, but her teeth below her braces were pointy and sharp. She really had been born in the wrong world.

I got a measurement problem that I immediately knew the answer to. I pretended to work on it a bit, but I knew my parents were on a time line, so I didn't belabor my explanation.

Willy's turn was next. Mr. Bartlett scowled as Willy chose an envelope.

"Statistics and Probability."

Easy out, I thought, as Willy read the problem aloud and began to chew on his bottom lip.

He was struggling, but he didn't give up. I watched impatiently. The answer was *so* obvious. I tried to think of Willy as food, a source of essence and nutrition, as Willy grabbed another overhead sheet and continued to work. His red hair curled over his shirt collar. I thought about how Willy wanted to impress me snowboarding, how he laughed at my jokes, and then I saw him smile.

"The answer is 157 to 1," he said, and he was right.

We were on the last round. Alicia was good in math, but the next probability problem was a killer.

She was given an overhead sheet to display with six cards drawn on it:

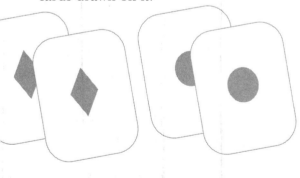

The directions at the bottom said:

What would the probability be of picking a diamond card and a circle card? The diamond is not returned before the circle card is chosen.

I glanced down to the audience while Alicia considered the problem. Mom gave me a little wave and then looked at her watch. I thought about how all her knowledge of probability didn't help her with the poker game in Reno. Random chance was like that. You could never be *absolutely* certain of the outcome. Some things were improbable, but did occur; for example, Willy being up on the stage tonight. Somehow he'd beaten the odds with help from Margie and me, but he'd also beaten them by studying and believing in himself.

Dad gave me a thumbs-up. What was the likelihood that Earth, at war with itself most of the time, could thwart a galactic power like the Home World? The odds weren't good, something like ten trillion to one. Numbers were on our side. Earth would be vanquished.

I was now living the last few hours in the world I'd always considered normal: family, friends, school, Prattville, California, the United States, the continent of North America, planet Earth. Soon, none of these things would have much meaning, as irrelevant to the future as Egyptian dynasties had been for me.

Grandmother's arms were crossed, but she was looking at Mr. Bartlett. Mr. Bartlett was looking back at her, a self-congratulatory smile on his face. How probable was it that the two strangers would communicate like that?

When Mr. Bartlett sneezed, had he said my real name, or did I just imagine he did? There really is only one way to say Dbkrrrsh, and whatever Mr. Bartlett had said sure sounded the way someone from home would pronounce it, accent on the "rrr" and everything. Things about Mr. Bartlett were starting to add up.

First of all, there was his love for raw food—but we

never saw him eat. Once Tony had asked if he ate raw steak, and Mr. Bartlett gave one of his rare smiles and said no. And Mr. Bartlett was never shy about how he hated teaching anything but math or science. So why wasn't he teaching high school?

Grandmother had told me that very afternoon that someone had been keeping tabs on me. Unless my parents were doing secret reports, someone else was watching. I looked back out to the audience just in time to catch Grandmother wink. She was either flirting, a thought too strange to be believed, or she was confirming my suspicions.

I decided to find out. I sneezed and said, "Mpfld."

My Bartlett's head whipped around. "Bless you," he said, as his mouth curved into a small smile. "There seems to be something in the air." His eyes locked with mine. "Something invasive."

I thought of the task ahead of me that night. My stomach felt so empty it hurt. My hunch had been verified. Willy shifted in the seat next to me, and I crossed my arms over my belly.

"I'd like to answer now," Alicia said petulantly. "The probability of the diamond card being picked is one-third." She was right so far. "And the probability of the circle card being picked is one-third."

Alicia had just lost the crown. She'd forgotten that the first card hadn't been put back. The correct answer for the circle card was 2/5. She was dead wrong.

"Sit down," Mr. Bartlett ordered her. He didn't even tell her "Good job."

Alicia blanched. If both Willy and I struck out, she'd get another turn, but she knew how good I was at math.

Mr. Bartlett called me up, and I picked an envelope. "Geometry," I announced after opening it. My task was to find the volume of a cone:

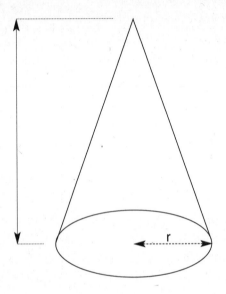

The formula for this is V = (BH)/3. I had to multiply the area of the base by the height, then divide by three. But first I needed to calculate the area of the base, which was πr^2.

I glanced at Willy, sitting nervously in his folding chair. A few weeks ago, no one would have thought he'd be here onstage. Willy had worked at something that was as natural to me as breathing. Would I really be a winner since my skill for math was genetic?

In his way, Willy had been just as honorable an opponent as Dog Girl. If he could figure out the next problem, he was the one who deserved the crown.

I "accidentally" forgot to square the radius.

I multiplied πr, not πr^2.

My mom and dad looked at each other in confusion. The scowl on Grandmother's face frightened me more than when she'd used the beauty treatment. But I'd made my choice.

Mr. Bartlett stood stunned, and then his eyes narrowed as he called Willy over to him. If Willy couldn't solve the next problem, I'd get another try and gladly win. But he deserved a chance.

Willy walked slowly to the overhead. He opened the envelope and stared at what he was supposed to do. Someone coughed in the audience, and he finally said, "Algebra, order of operations. Did you know that algebra is like a language?"

He picked up the pen, chewed on his bottom lip, and went to work on the overhead. He went off on a wrong tangent for a minute, but then crossed out what he'd written and started over.

$$3n/4 + 6(n+2) = 17$$
$$3n/4 + 6n + 12 = 17$$
$$(3/4 + 6)n + 12 = 17$$
$$6\ 3/4n + 12 = 17$$
$$6\ 3/4n + 12 - 12 = 17 - 12$$
$$6\ 3/4n = 5$$
$$(4/27 \times 27/4) \times n = 5 \times 4/27$$
$$n = 4/27 \times 5$$
$$n = 20/27$$

Willy announced in a voice more confident than I'd ever heard him use before, "The answer is n equals twenty over twenty-seven."

Mr. Bartlett's eyebrows arched in consternation. "Correct."

He reluctantly placed the Math Champ Crown on Willy's head. A huge cheer rose from the cafeteria. Dracula Boy had won the Math Champ Crown. My friend was going to die happy.

Willy was soon mobbed by the audience. Margie and Fred pushed through the crowd and gave him a big hug. Alicia hung back, resisting her parents' attempts to comfort her.

Mr. Bartlett grabbed my shoulder and pulled me behind the stage curtains, where Grandmother was waiting. Each of their tentacles extended one at a time until I was surrounded by twelve sets of razor-sharp teeth. I was surprised by how natural Mr. Bartlett looked with them poking out of his head. He was one of us, that was for sure.

"You dare to lose?" Grandmother asked.

Mr. Bartlett echoed her menacing tone. "You dare to shame your species?"

One of Grandmother's tentacles was pink and wrinkly, what mine might look like in ninety years. She extended it close to my face, so all I could see was the saw-toothed pattern of its teeth, the thin sinewy tongue, and the darkness that led to her stomach.

My legs were shaking. I needed food. "I got the idea," I said.

"Sentimentality is an unnecessary emotion," Mr. Bartlett told me.

Grandmother continued with my scolding. "You have let down the entire House of Mfpld. I've had my doubts of your trustworthiness from the reports Brltt has sent over the years." She indicated Mr. Bartlett with a nod in his direction. "After your performance during your purgation, I thought things might be different, but you have proven yourself to be kind to the humans once again."

"Do not disappoint us again," Mr. Bartlett said. Both his and Grandmother's tentacles retracted. "You were supposed to win tonight."

Alicia opened the curtains just in time for her and Willy, who stood next to her, to hear these last words. The two of them glared at me.

"Alicia thought you lost on purpose," he said. "I didn't believe her until now."

"But Willy," I said. "I—"

He cut off my words. "I thought I won on my own tonight. Thanks for nothing."

He turned around and marched off. I pushed Alicia to the side and followed, but Margie stepped in my way.

"Fred's gone on to the theater, and your parents said they had to run, but Virginia left your costume with me. Do you mind changing in the girls' bathroom so we can leave?"

As I walked into the bathroom, Alicia walked out in a violet vampiress dress.

"Serves you right, Deborah," she said.

I said nothing. In a few short hours, I'd get my revenge.

Chapter Seventeen

Dbkmsh

With Willy's saxophone in the trunk, he, Alicia, and I were jammed in the backseat of Margie's car. I was dressed in the same silver jumpsuit I'd worn on Halloween for the wedding. My tentacles were all fully extended, each jaw clamped tight, resisting how sweet it would be to spill blood then and there. Sentimentality *was* an unnecessary emotion.

"Did you know that I was the spelling bee champion for the entire school district? Not to mention I already have a crown for gymnastics," Alicia said. She was still in a state of unbelief about not winning Math Champs. "I would never lose a competition on purpose the way Deborah did."

I imagined that Mr. Bartlett had told her to expect to win just to increase her flavor of betrayal.

"That's enough, Alicia," Margie said. She eyed me in the rearview mirror, her eyes squinting the way they did sometimes when she was worried.

Willy had these little bolts in his neck and his hair in a Frankenstein 'do. His outfit was a little too small for him, just like the monster in the poster on his parents' refrigerator. Even though he was furious at me, I liked his scars. A lot.

SENTIMENTALITY IS A WASTED EMOTION!!!!!

The words screamed so loudly in my head I hardly had room for my tentacles.

I focused back on blood and guts and then tried to picture Gerald with bolts in his neck, like an extreme sort of piercing. I remembered the look he gave me when I'd finished my purgation. That was an experience Willy couldn't even come close to fathoming. Thinking about it made my hunger almost unbearable.

Grandmother had kept her plans a secret. Gerald was in Nevada fiddling with all the communication devices and sending signals to Mom. Dad had driven with Stan to the Sacramento Airport, the designated landing place for our area.

All of the planes were just going to be zapped to make way for our airships. Poof! Now you see them, now you don't. I imagined citizens of Earth dumbstruck as thousands of lights descended from the sky and multitentacle-eating beings—my species—surged forth.

"Guess what?" Alicia said, interrupting my thoughts. "We're going to Disney World as soon as school is out this year." *Great,* I thought. *She can ride Space Mountain with Our Most Supreme Imperial High Matriarch. I guess Disneyland wasn't good enough for either of them.* A few seconds later, Alicia's voice turned into sugar. "Margie, could Willy go?"

"I don't think so," Margie said.

"Why not?" Alicia asked.

"Willy's too young to go all the way across the country without his family. Maybe sometime your family and ours could go to Disneyland together. We could vacation down there."

Alicia looked even more vexed.

There was dead silence in the car for the next few miles. Margie turned off the freeway and merged onto a wide street full of traffic. She drove into a parking garage, unsnapped her seat belt, and turned around to face us.

"Willy, is there something you need to say to Deborah?" she asked.

Willy sat impassively. I couldn't believe how stubborn he was. He was the human, so I wasn't going to be the first to talk.

"William Dylan Logan," Margie said.

Tears started to pour down his face. My tentacles drooped when I saw them. I took a deep breath. *Essence. Conquering. Snowboarding. Hungry. Red tears—not good.* I managed to blink away my own tears to focus on the job I had to do. Willy turned his head toward Alicia, who had put in her plastic fangs.

All of us sat there uncomfortably for about a minute until finally he burst out with "She didn't think I was smart enough to win on my own. I'll never know if I could have really won all by myself."

"Then tell *her* how you feel," Margie said.

Willy looked like he was about to spit in my face. "I'd rather have lost than won this way."

Margie handed him a tissue and he blew his nose.

"You don't understand," I said. "It wasn't like that at all."

Margie sighed and looked at her watch. "We're late."

We all got out, and Margie popped the trunk. Willy pulled out his saxophone case.

Alicia took out her fangs so she could talk. "You're not going to torture the audience with that?"

A little smile erupted on her face as if to say "I'm just teasing." Instead, the smile made her remark seem especially cruel.

Willy looked at Margie.

"I told you I don't want to do this," he said.

"Nonsense," Margie said. "You did great at the rehearsal. The film needs your music."

The three of us followed Margie up the stairs to the street and across to the theater.

"The Crest isn't just a theater," Margie said when we walked in. "This place was built in the nineteen-twenties in a style called Art Deco, and people back then called it a movie palace. Just look at all the details."

The foyer had rose-colored walls and plush carpet of brown and gold brocade. Circling over our heads like a huge tiara, bronze leaves and vines decorated the ceiling's rim. At least a hundred freaky people were milling about.

Margie was wearing her beautiful black wedding dress again, and she sailed through the lobby like she was the queen of the dead. Vampires of all kinds, traditional and goth, several Freddy Kruegers, an assortment of witches and wizards, aliens (the fake kind), and a couple of really creepy mummies parted so that we could make our way to the candy counter.

Before Margie went to find Fred, she handed Willy a twenty-dollar bill and told us to get what we wanted.

"My parents have become kind of famous," Willy told Alicia as we lined up behind a ghost completely covered in white silk. He was still ignoring me, but at least he'd stopped crying. "The news of the lawsuit actually helped the business at Dad's video store. We've heard that people have come to the film festival from as far away as Seattle."

He put down his case as the ghost stepped up to the counter.

"You're really going to play?" I asked. "I think that's great."

Willy didn't answer my question, but at least he said something to me.

"Do you want anything?"

Alicia's liver, I thought. "No, I'm back on the diet."

Willy crinkled up his nose and then got the largest container of popcorn he could buy, four different kinds of candy bars, and two sodas.

"This should last us until *The Blob* comes on," he said, handing Alicia her soda.

A headless giant walked past us, dribbles of red acrylic paint flowing down the stump of his neck. I lost control of my pink tentacle, and it started to hover over Alicia's head, drooling on it. She looked up, and I dropped some saliva in her eye.

"You're not only a loser, Deborah, you're really gross," she said, wiping frantically at her face and running into the bathroom.

Willy stood on tiptoe and looked at the top of my head.

"Your tentacles are so cool. They look like they're

coming right out of your skull. Could I borrow them sometime?" he asked.

"I thought you were mad at me," I said.

"I am," he said.

"Willy, you deserve the crown. You've improved in math more than anyone. Nobody helped you with that equation. You did it all yourself."

He didn't say anything for a long moment, and then he told me something that I loved hearing.

"Deborah, I don't like Alicia, but my parents have told me I have to be nice to her. They think being nice to her family will make things easier on me at school, but I can't stand how she hangs on me."

"You're not her boyfriend?" I asked.

"Oh, please," Willy said.

If I didn't have to kill him later, I think I'd have kissed him. Instead, my stomach growled.

"Are you okay?" Willy asked. "You look sort of goofy."

Before I could say anything else, Alicia was back.

"If you ever do something like that to me again, I'll punch you."

"Like I'm really scared, Alicia," I said.

Margie and Fred found us. Margie looked like she was wondering what she was thinking when she asked Alicia and me both along for the evening. Fred was oblivious of the tension. He'd shaved his head and wore some sort of makeup that made him look like he was three days' dead.

"You're ready, son?"

Willy nodded. "I'll see you later," he said, handing me his soda and all of the candy bars. "Keep these safe."

He followed Fred through the gilded doors that led into the auditorium.

"I'm so glad we talked him into playing tonight," Margie said.

Alicia's nose curled up like a caterpillar. I could just see her whispering to Amanda at school on Wednesday. Neither of them appreciated jazz.

But there wasn't going to be school on Wednesday. The invasion was solving so many of my problems.

"We saved you seats in the first row of the balcony," Margie said. "Willy will be on in a few minutes to get things rolling. Why don't you girls go in? Fred and I are going to watch from backstage."

I felt as if I'd stepped into a palace. The walls were shades of rose, and above us, the ceiling was like the most beautiful night sky you could imagine, deep blues and lavenders and lights that shone like stars, all of this trimmed with heavy bronze reliefs. I had never seen curtains in a movie theater before, but here thick golden ones hung in front of the screen, and in front of them was a real stage for Willy. The theater was enormous. Our Most Supreme Imperial High Matriarch was going to be pleased.

Our seats had red ribbons with the word RESERVED printed on them. Alicia moved over to the third one and I sat on the aisle. Willy would just have to sit between us when he came back.

I looked at my watch. It was almost 8:00. The first invaders from the airships would be down soon. Almost all the seats were filled. The festival was going to be a success. Grandmother would be pleased.

I practiced saying Hrthr-vtck to myself, finally getting it right on the fifth attempt. Pronouncing this the right way was more important than thinking about how much I hated Alicia. I'd be meeting Her Majesty in a few hours. I wouldn't have the Math Champ Crown, but I still could impress her and help my family secure a good position in the coming new Earth. I crossed my fingers and made a wish that I wouldn't call Grandmother Pig's Butt in front of her.

I hoped somehow Willy's family would appreciate five hundred hungry aliens bursting into the theater just at the moment in the movie when the Blob crashes through the projectionist's screen and eats everyone in sight. We might be bloodthirsty, but Dad always said we were a species with a sense of humor.

The ghost from the candy line squeezed in front of me to sit next to Alicia. The lights all went out except for a single spotlight that lit up the area around the microphone.

Fred stepped out from behind the curtain, and everyone broke into applause. Several people whistled. He motioned for everyone to be quiet.

"Tonight will be a night like no other Sacramento has ever experienced," he said. "I promise that by the time you leave here in the early hours tomorrow morning, you will have experienced terror like you never have before in your life. The first feature is the only surviving portion of the film *Dracula Wept*, made in Romania in 1914."

A loud cheer came up from all around me in the dark. Willy stepped onstage in his Frankenstein costume, his saxophone hanging from around his neck.

The curtains slowly drew back, and all the lights went out. Complete silence, and then Willy blew a high squeaky note on his sax that made me jump three inches out of my seat. Maybe Alicia was right about Willy this time, and he was planning to torture the audience.

A grainy black-and-white field of waving grass was projected onto the screen. Slowly the scene darkened and turned into night. *Dracula Wept* was an old silent film, the kind where an organist would play music in the theater to accompany it. We got Willy instead because it was his parents' festival.

A low moan came from his sax as a bat flew across the screen. Dracula, of course. The bat flew to a gypsy camp where a dark, wild-haired young woman danced in front of a fire. Willy's sax began to sound like someone was crying. He knew exactly what he was doing. Total improvisation, nothing like any gypsy music I'd ever heard, but perfect for the scene. I started to wonder if he were possessed, if his family had their own dark secret, like they really were vampires. What were those coffins doing in their living room anyway?

The clip ended with the bat transforming into Dracula, standing menacingly in the shadows of the fire, the girl whirling into the cape that he was raising. Willy's music was perfectly matched, catching both the horror and the sadness of the scene.

The lights came on again and the audience whistled and cheered. Willy smiled and then turned and walked offstage.

Alicia leaned toward me, across Willy's seat. "Everyone feels sorry for him. He really was awful."

"Alicia, if you say another word, I'm going to drool on you again," I said.

"Just try it," she said, and then stepped hard on my foot as she walked out to the aisle.

I was starving, and I couldn't wait any longer. It was time for her to die. I'd tell Willy that she got a call on her cell phone, and her parents came to pick her up early. Dog Girl had been a worthy meal, but Alicia was true humanoid scum and the sooner she was gone, the better.

I followed her into the ladies' room. No one else was there. Perfect. It was time for Alicia to be sacrificed. I was ready. I was eager. Once I got rid of her, Willy would be . . . a necessary sacrifice.

Alicia's feet showed below the door of a stall. I braced myself on the sink across from her and closed my eyes. I imagined myself back in the Desolation Area, and I remembered the pain I'd felt there and the glory as I triumphed over Dog Girl.

The toilet flushed, and I opened my eyes. Each of my tentacles was ready, eighteen rows of sharp teeth were prepared to rip into her as soon as the door opened. I'd get her before she even stepped out of the stall. There was nothing in my life I had ever wanted to do more, and I was very hungry.

I lunged as soon as I heard Alicia unlock the door, just as the ghost, who seemed to be following us, walked in. Alicia had just a second to see my six tentacles heading straight for her body before I clamped them shut. I fell on top of her, knocking her back onto the toilet seat.

If nothing else, I finally managed to shut her up. The

ghost acted like she hadn't seen anything and went into the stall next to the one we were tangled up in. My tentacles were wrapped around Alicia. I pried them away and pushed myself off of her. She sat there stunned, holding onto the toilet seat.

I'd scared her big time. Good. She was going to be particularly tasty once I got over my embarrassment for being so clumsy.

I left her there and walked back out to the lobby. Was the ghost really following me? I didn't care. It didn't matter because very soon nothing on Earth was going to be a problem.

Willy was standing next to a huge cardboard figure of Hannibal Lecter.

"Where were you?" he asked, "*The Blob* is going to start in just a few minutes."

Alicia emerged from the bathroom. Her vampire dress had ripped and her hair looked like she was getting ready to have dreadlocks.

"Are you all right?" Willy asked.

I made my choice. I had to do it. Now.

"Alicia's not feeling that great," I said. "Let's go outside and get some air before the movie starts."

"I don't want to go outside," Alicia protested, but I grabbed her arm and pulled her through the lobby and out the theater door. Several people were standing in line for tickets, so I took hold of Willy, too, and marched the three of us to an alley that ran next to the building and shoved them both up against the wall.

"What are you doing?" Willy asked.

My grip tightened.

Alicia tried to pull away, but I was strong and I was

hungry. The real Frankenstein wouldn't have escaped me. "You're hurting me. Let me go," Alicia cried. Panic crept into her voice, delicious like a marinade on a steak.

I was so much stronger than the two of them, so much superior. Power was everything, just like my family said. I decided to kill Willy fast and clean, so that he wouldn't have to suffer. By killing him quickly I wouldn't get the full taste of betrayal, but he was my friend, after all.

But then I'd toy with Alicia. She would be so scared that she'd be more delectable than Dog Girl by the time I was done with her.

I bared each set of teeth one at a time. Willy's eyes widened and he swallowed hard. I stepped back. One of my tentacles all by itself took a snip at Alicia's shoulder. I tasted her blood, so very sweet for such a sour personality. She tried to scream, but another tentacle hovered an inch away from her mouth and seemed to suck her voice out of her.

"Deborah?" Willy asked in confusion, so scared he could only whisper.

"I'm not Deborah. I'm Dbkrrrsh," I said with more determination than I had ever felt, but then from nowhere I felt the tears coming. It was all I could do to keep the half of my tentacles that wanted to devour Alicia in check and the other half that didn't want to eat Willy ready to attack.

I took a deep breath and made myself stop crying. I wasn't going to shed sloppy red tears again. No more of this, ever. Willy was just a human, not worth crying over.

"I'm sorry, Willy," I said. "My species is coming tonight."

I forced my three tentacles toward his throat, his heart, and his stomach. One snap with each and it would be all over quickly, and then I could concentrate on Alicia. I would finally become who I really was, Dbkrrrsh all the way through.

"Good-bye, Willy," I said, and opened my jaws wide.

Chapter Eighteen

Tentacles

I felt Willy's breath on my gums. I was that close to him. I could smell his sweat as it mixed with the alley smells: the garbage in the cans a few feet off, cigarette butts scattered on the ground, a broken whiskey bottle that lay near Alicia's feet.

My tongue closest to Willy's head took on a life of its own and licked his face. Our tongues are coarse, like cats', and I felt him wince. I wondered how my breath smelled. I hoped not bad. I'd hate for that to be the last thing Willy thought of.

My jaws were aching. I needed to bite down hard. All it would take would be that first bite and this conflict inside me would be over.

"Don't!" a woman's voice called out behind me. "Don't do it, Deborah."

My pink tentacle whipped around. I kept the other five trained on Willy and Alicia, who was trying to scream underneath my hand. I looked out of the corner of my eye.

The ghost again.

"If you don't stop now, your life will be ruined," she said behind her hood.

"You don't know anything about it," I said.

I was going to have to finish her off, too. She'd be easy, someone I didn't know. It would be like feeding on Halloween.

"Please, Deborah. Listen to me."

I knew who she was then, Agent Mackenzie. I hesitated. She sensed it and took a step forward.

"Don't do that," I yelled.

Willy's face was being bathed in my saliva. He tried to shake it off, and one of my teeth scratched his cheek. The taste of blood, the taste of his fear, seeped into me. Willy's blood made me want to forget he was my friend, and that I'd planned to be merciful.

"The invasion isn't going to happen," Agent Mackenzie said.

I froze.

"How do you know about the invasion?" I asked.

"Watch me," she said.

I looked at her, knowing the wait would make the kill even better.

Her hood rose two feet in the air.

"You don't have to follow the old ways. You have a choice. We've been watching you and know how you've tried to change."

What was I seeing? I stared at her hard. And then I saw them below the hem of the hood. Tentacles. And one of them was pink like mine, a sure sign that this stranger was a female from the House of Mfpld. She was my species, my own flesh and blood, yet she was telling me not to feed. I didn't understand.

"But the essence," I said. "And I'm so hungry."

She nodded to show me she understood and lowered her tentacles, taking off her hood as they came down. "Yes, I remember the essence, but the longer you do without it, the easier it gets. There are no vitamins in it. That's just propaganda from the Home World. Essence is just great-tasting empty calories. There will come a day when you hardly think about it at all. Other things, like doing the right thing, making the decision not to kill, will become more important."

I didn't believe her. I wanted Willy's essence now, and then Alicia's. I wanted it more than I'd even wanted Dog Girl's.

"The essence," I repeated, longing for it to flow through me.

"Your parents want you to live for the order, for the approval of the Supreme High Council," she said, "but there's another way."

"How do you know?" I asked.

"It's the programming we've all had. Your grand-mother saw to that." She looked away for a moment, a foolish gesture on her part, but I was too confused to use her distraction to attack. "There's a small group of us that have broken away. We've followed your parents to Earth to protect it and hope someday to be able to make changes in our culture. I've always hoped the first people to change would be your family."

My parents were wrong. There really was a resis-tance.

Alicia struggled so hard I was afraid I was going to

have to suffocate her. Willy stood stock-still and mute. He didn't need hair gel to keep his hair standing on end anymore.

"Why my family?" I asked.

"Because I'm your aunt, Dbkrrrsh. Your mother's little sister. Let the kids go."

I couldn't. I had my duty to perform, my parents to not disappoint, my grandmother to deal with, all the history and genetics of my species behind me to do this very thing.

"I don't believe you."

"Right now the ships are being thrown off by a force field surrounding this planet and hurled halfway across the galaxy toward home," said Agent Mackenzie, or my aunt, or whoever she was. "Those of us in the resistance have been able to assume a lot of power in places where it makes the biggest difference for the defense of Earth."

Alicia bit my hand. One of my tentacles slapped her.

I sucked on the blood breaking through my skin. My own blood. My heart stopped racing. All the strength left my body. I let Willy and Alicia go.

"If you tell anyone about this, my parents will eat your parents and I'll eat you."

Both of them stood like mannequins.

"*The Blob* has started by now," my aunt said. She really was my aunt. There was something in her voice that was too much like my mother's for her not to be related to us. "Why don't the two of you go inside?"

Willy and Alicia slid across the wall and then ran around the corner.

"I won't arrest your parents if you promise not to feed anymore. We'll keep close tabs on Vgnrlk and

Grrgg, as well as the two young men staying with you. They won't be able to feed again."

Vgnrlk. Grrgg. My parents. It was so strange to hear their real names.

"They'll starve then," I said, slumping to the ground, almost sitting on the whiskey bottle. "Why didn't you stop us before? We've fed every year."

"Your parents are very clever, Deborah," she said, using my Earth name, the one I liked best. "It wasn't until I found your family in Reno that I knew where they were. The powder Grandmother put in the passport was what alerted me. I researched unusual deaths and disappearances and the pattern was just too close to what I knew from home. It wasn't easy squelching the rumor about it being alien DNA, by the way.

"We never suspected Jimmy Joe Crawford would be a victim, but if we had arrested your grandmother after he died, the Home World would have known something was up. They might have invaded early, before we were ready to deflect them."

"Just so you know, Mom didn't have anything to do with Jimmy Joe," I said.

"Your grandmother deserves all the blame." My aunt's voice became icy. "Your family has fed only to survive and because they've been brainwashed, but she is truly evil, even for the Home World."

"And Mr. Bartlett's not exactly in the diplomatic corps," I said.

She nodded. "We thought there was another agent. I did a background check. He's been Mother's accomplice for more than one invasion."

I was getting cold in the alley. I began to shiver. I

pulled in my tentacles, and so did she.

"But why didn't Mom and Grandmother know who you were," I asked.

"The last time Mother saw me I didn't look like this," she said, pointing to her face.

"You've got a great sense of fashion," I said.

"Thank you," she said. "Deborah, Vgnrlk doesn't know anything about me. She was away at school when I was born, and Mother . . . well, that's not a story I want to tell now. We've sent some of our best people to arrest both her and Brltt. What I want is for you to help me with your family, convince them not to feed anymore, so we won't have to be heavy-handed with them next fall."

"What about Stan and Gerald?" I asked.

"Yes, they seem like nice young men. Maybe they can be convinced, too."

"This isn't going to be easy," I told her.

"We have until next Halloween, don't we?" She gave me her hand and pulled me up. "Deborah, you can't tell them who I am. This has to be our secret."

"Why?" I asked.

"Because our species is very clever, and from what I know from our operatives who are in deep cover aboard the ships, they're starving. They'll be back. I need to stay undercover to prepare for that day."

My aunt put her hood back over her head. "Let's go inside and get some popcorn before the Blob attacks the theater," she said. "It's my favorite part of the movie."

Driving home was really strange. I think Margie was pleased by how polite Alicia had gotten all of a sudden, but when I walked in the front door, it felt like *Night of the*

Living Dead. Everyone looked depressed.

"There were problems, dear," Mom said.

I didn't say a word about Grandmother not being there, and neither did anyone else. I flossed because there was popcorn lodged in my teeth, the only set I was going to need from here on out. I went to bed still hungry, but I had plans to meet Willy at Burger King the next day for lunch.

A week later, Aunt Susan contacted me. She asked me only to call her Aunt Susan in private. She'd gone to Alicia's house and left a few *Watchtower* magazines. When her parents brought them inside, a powder not unlike the one my family had used at the Lucky Nugget spread through the house. Alicia forgot all about the night before, and her parents didn't remember the crazy story their daughter had told them about aliens, tentacles, and almost being eaten by her classmate Deborah.

I begged Aunt Susan not to erase Willy's memory. I told her we could trust him 100 percent, and that I needed someone to talk to when she wasn't around. She was reluctant, but then the three of us met at Burger King to discuss the matter.

She told him about the seriousness of the situation. Somehow Grandmother and Mr. Bartlett had slipped away and evaded arrest. They were out there somewhere, plotting and calculating. The good news is that Ms. Martinez is our teacher now!

She's respectful to all of us, though I think Willy might be her favorite. She always gives him a big smile when he answers questions. Willy's become quite the good student, though I wouldn't be surprised if she was a little charmed by those eyes of his.

Aunt Susan said Willy would be watched very closely. He understands that, if he breathes a word of her cover, or of aliens on Earth, or even mentions the word *tentacles* to someone other than to me, his memory will be erased.

I've apologized for almost eating him, and he's taken it pretty well. In fact, he actually thinks knowing a real live alien is cool. We've started to collect information about UFOs, and he has stacks of magazines about them next to his coffin.

Willy's sworn that my origin will remain our secret, but every so often he asks to see my tentacles. I tell him it's dangerous, but he doesn't seem to mind. So far I've grazed him only once when two of them got out of control.

Memories of Dog Girl are always with me. I try to have something in my stomachs when I see him so I won't be tempted to munch on one of his fingers or take an ear off. If I did that, I'm not sure if I could stop myself. I don't tell him that, though.

I'm not hiding what I'm eating anymore. Mom especially hates it.

"She's going through a stage," Dad said a few days ago when they found a pint of Chunky Monkey in the freezer. "If we keep telling her no, she'll want to eat more."

Mom shook her head and walked out of the kitchen. Dad took off the top of the carton and stared at the ice cream.

"Want a bite?" I asked, pulling a plastic spoon out from a drawer.

Dad put the lid back on and chuckled. "I'm not that easy to trick," he said.

Grandmother and Mr. Bartlett may have vanished from the face of the Earth. Were they beamed back aboard a ship? Are they hiding out someplace even more remote than the Oasis? Aunt Susan says they might still be in Northern California, living in disguise. No one knows, but I have a feeling we haven't seen the last of them.

Dad is trying to figure out how Earth governments developed the force field. He can't find any information on it. He's frustrated, plus he still has his boring accounting job. We were left with that huge credit-card bill for the Hummer.

He still dreams of running a pro shop at a golf course someday. When I asked about his wanting to be a ski park manager, he said that when it comes down to it, golf is his true love, but he's promised to take me up to the Sierras again before winter is over.

Mom has been down in the dumps. She plays Jimmy Joe Crawford CDs morning, noon, and night, but last week she finally attended a Garden Club meeting with Margie, and it seemed to cheer her up. She planted a rosebush yesterday and Dad says that's a sign she'll be feeling better soon.

I'm still engaged, I guess, but nobody has said anything more about it. I treat Gerald like an older brother at this point. He's going to the community college and found out he has a flair for acting. He's appearing in a production based on *Silence of the Lambs* and gets to be Hannibal, himself. Stan joked that it was typecasting, but we're all proud of him.

Stan plays golf with Dad. He got a job at a Radio Shack in Rancho Cordova, and he's started to date one of the other salesclerks. My parents, of course, don't approve because they remember the girl he's betrothed to.

I'm biting my tongues not to tell Mom who Aunt Susan is because I think the news might perk her up, but Aunt Susan keeps telling me that now is not the time.

Aunt Susan did finally let me know what happened when she was a baby. After she'd had a particularly fussy day, Grandmother offered her as a snack to a Supreme High Council member. The council member had just fed, but he didn't want to be rude. He took Aunt Susan off Grandmother's hands and gave her to a childless family about to board a ship leaving the Home World. When Aunt Susan became an adult, after her purgation on the frog planet, she was told everything.

A few months before she was to marry her fiancé (a distant cousin she'd never met), she fell in love with another young man in the resistance. Eventually she escaped to Earth with him and some others. I asked her to tell me her real vowel-less name, but she wouldn't and said that she left that person behind a long time ago.

My parents have been spending a lot of time with the Impala in the garage. Stan told me another invasion is being planned. I feel a little bit like a spy, but Aunt Susan says the Home World will always be a threat. She says our side has to be vigilant.

Other than that, things have been pretty slow. There's that report on the Aztecs I need to write, but I'm finally feeling a connection with social studies.

The Aztecs played a game like basketball and the losing team had their hearts ripped out. I'm wondering if my species might have made an earlier visit to Earth.

There's a game that's similar back home.

I'm getting hungry again, so I guess that's about it. I'm going to my favorite deli for a pork loin sandwich. One thing's for sure: when I have to eat, I really have to eat.